CAIN'S CROSS

Bullard's Battle
Book #2

Dale Mayer

CAIN'S CROSS (BULLARD'S BATTLE, BOOK 2)
Dale Mayer
Valley Publishing

ISBN-13: 978-1-773363-22-6
Print Edition

Books in This Series:

About This Book

Welcome to a new stand-alone but interconnected series from Dale Mayer. This is Bullard's story—and that of his team's. All raw, rough, incredibly capable men who have one goal: to find out who was behind the attack on their leader, before the attacker, or attackers, return to finish the job.

Stay tuned for more nonstop action as the men narrow down their suspects … and find a way to let love back into their own empty lives.

Cain—hearing a killer's last words, "You're next,"—knows his time is running out, not only for him but for his entire team. As members of his team search for the still missing Bullard in the ocean, Cain has focused on tracking the killer's history, hopefully to lead to the madman after them all. A trip to Sicily brings more information to light but also more puzzles to sort out. And an unexpected light in Cain's life.

When Petra picks up the two men at the airport, she has no idea how fast her personal life is about to unravel. Not only do these men bring up old terrible memories but they also shine a light on an ugly corner of town. People she avoids at all costs.

Still she can't afford to dwell on the past, as her present blows up. With Cain and Eton at her side, they're all trying to stay alive, as the bodies drop around them.

CHAPTER 1

I T HAD BEEN several weeks since the shooting at the museum that had sent Ryland back to the hospital. Now that he was safely out at sea with Tabi and enjoying his life, Eton Duram and Cain Bestrow had gone dark, hiding, while they figured out what in the hell they would do next. They knew it was all about gathering intel at this point, and, since they had a solid plan, it was time to make a move.

But just because Cain had plans in mind didn't mean their opponents didn't have plans of their own. Cain couldn't forget the last words of one of the gunmen they'd taken out at the art gallery with Ryland.

"Cain, you're next."

So not only had Green's goons known who Ryland was, they'd also known who Cain was, and the gunmen had made it very clear that killing Bullard was part of their plan. So, taking him out—along with the rest of the team—was all part and parcel of the same deal. Cain still had no word on Bullard, after his plane had been downed, dumping him and Ryland and Garret in the ocean. It ate at Cain to think of that strong and majestic man out there suffering.

Bullard would deal with it in his usual stoic way, but he would also know that his team would be looking for him. Even now four of them still went up and down the coast, checking the small islands, speaking to the local fishermen and talking to the natives to ensure that nobody had seen Bullard or had picked him up accidentally. Or picked him up and helped him but hadn't told the authorities, for whatever reason. Cain had absolutely no proof that Bullard had been picked up and knew it was all too likely he'd become fish food, but that was something impossible to reconcile with a six-foot-six 260-pound powerhouse.

But everybody died sometime, even Bullard.

Cain stood here, staring out the window of the Swiss chalet high up in the Alps; not a place most people expected him to go, but he needed to go underground, and here he was. Garret was at least awake now; not necessarily doing very well, but he was awake and aware. It had taken him days, but, once he'd come out of the coma, everything had seemed to go so much easier in Garret's recovery. He'd started healing much faster too. It would be at least a couple weeks before he was well enough to join the fight, but he was eager, willing, and actually pissed off at being held back. Yet he had agreed to recuperate, as was Ryland, for the time being.

In the meantime, Garret was in the hospital, waiting for the swelling on his brain to stabilize. He had also suffered several other fractures, and they needed to heal up as well. A few more days and he could leave the hospital and recuperate elsewhere. So, while Garret and Ryland recovered from their injuries, Cain had Eton at his side.

He turned to see his old friend with spreadsheets all over the place. "You and your spreadsheets," Cain said, shaking his head.

"I could say the same about you and your blueprints, you know?" Eton shook his head.

"At least my paperwork gets us in and out of buildings."

"And mine is getting us in and out of bank accounts," Eton said, laughing.

"Have to give you that one," Cain muttered because that's what Eton was doing—sorting money, seeing who was moving money where.

They had tracked down as many of the gunmen involved in Ryland's case as they could. Then they had tracked the money trail. And definitely money had been flowing. When Green—the guy who set up the big finale in the museum—went down, his life had become an open book, and the team had gone through it with a fine-tooth comb, looking at every account and connection to see how he was hired, who did it, and why.

It was the *why* that kept poking at the team because, without a *why*, none of the rest of it made any sense. They were just so close but couldn't find anything they could hold on to. They had plenty of old cases that gave them a big list of suspects. They had again sorted through the initial nineteen cases with the most likely perps—minus the five dead and the one in a coma—where they thought someone might have viable reasons, resources, and the means to come after Bullard and his team. Now they'd whittled those thirteen cases down to seven.

The father who'd lost his daughter on one of Bullard's missions was one of the possible suspects. Particularly since two of his men had come to work for Bullard for a time and then went back to working with the father—as if checking out Bullard's team for its weaknesses and strengths, collecting intel for their boss. So, there was always a chance the mastermind behind this attack on Bullard and his team was this father, who sought vengeance for the death of his daughter by kidnappers. Unfortunately Bullard's team had arrived too late to save her. Cain and Eton had finally located the father, named Groner, and he currently lived just outside of Dubai.

But where was he at any other time? Who knew? His face was a permanent fixture associated with the media company he handled. The problem was the timing. It just didn't make a whole lot of sense why he would do this now. It was one thing to wait for an opportunity, but it was another thing to choose an opportunity this far down the road. It had been at least one year ago since his daughter had died in captivity. Maybe even longer than that. It was amazing how time flew by when you were having fun. And since when did visiting Ice and Levi constitute a weakness or provide the opportunity for an attack?

Because Bullard flew all over the place. Or did someone just happen to have contacts in Houston that Groner could pull from? Or even anywhere in America actually because Houston was just another one of a zillion mega-airports around the world.

But small private planes didn't go in through the same areas as the big planes even in the same airports. The small planes always had their separate hangars and small runways to get in and out, making it a little easier for people to come and sabotage a seemingly innocuous flight. It also made these smaller planes easier to find, as often less security was involved, and that was one of the things that blew Cain away. If someone would spend that kind of money on a private plane, wouldn't it make sense to have sufficient security around to protect it? But typically there wasn't. The big airports were always looking for terrorists and people smuggling drugs in and out. But, for the small private planes, it just wasn't the same, and that fact was a reality Cain and his team had come to accept. Now, as Cain sat here in the chalet, overlooking the mountains all around him, he awaited answers.

Answers that weren't coming.

"Are you ready to leave?" Eton asked.

"I was ready to leave two days ago," Cain bit off. "You know we're waiting for answers."

"I don't think we'll find them here," Eton said casually.

"We're obviously not finding them at all," Cain said and turned to glare at his buddy. "Anytime you think you have a better idea, let me know."

"I think we should go on the offensive," Eton said.

"And how will we do that?" he asked, his stance spread slightly wider.

"Not sure, but I still think it's time. We need to move."

"As soon as we get the answers."

"They won't tell us anything," Eton said easily. He got up, stretched his arms, reaching toward the massive beams above.

"Sicily?"

"It's the last known place for this Green guy—or at least his two dead goons, Chico and that other guy," Eton replied.

"And yet," Cain said, "it doesn't tell us anything."

"We know nobody's been seen around or going into Chico's apartment lately. We know that the local authorities don't have a criminal file on him. We know that he has family there. And in France."

"So we'll track down this Chico's lifestyle?"

"We've done what we can online," Eton said. "Now it's time to pound on a few doors." Just then Eton's phone rang. "Bingo." He picked it up, smiled, and said, "What have you got for me?" He knew that, on their team, everybody was pulling in as much information as they could.

The man on the phone replied, "Ticket info has been sent to you. Pedro will pick you up at the airport."

"Fine. And then what?" Eton asked.

"You've been booked into a small bed-and-breakfast at the edge of town," he said. "The family has connections to your target." With that, he hung up.

"Good enough," Eton said, turning to Cain. "We have a place to stay in Sicily, and it's with a family related, well, connected to our target, Chico."

At that, Cain raised his eyebrows. "Is that wise?"

"Depends on whether they know why we're there or not," he said cheerfully. "But being strangers is a good way to get to know the area, and the hosts of those B&B places always try to be friendly."

"Until they find out you killed their family member," Cain said.

Eton looked at him, laughed, and said, "Well, there is that."

"And who's this Pedro character?"

"No clue," Eton said. "We'll find out."

Cain walked to where his bag was, ready to go as it had been every morning. While they flew out, the beds at the B&B would need to be changed, so their rooms wouldn't be ready right away. Meanwhile Cain also had a stack of paperwork to deal with. He stood with his phone on Camera mode and quickly took photographs of everything he needed, then put the rest into the fireplace and lit a match to it.

"Hey, not everybody has your photographic memory, you know?" Eton grumbled.

"You can keep your spreadsheets and bring them with

us," he said, "but we can't afford to have these blueprints found."

"And yet, to a layperson, they're just blueprints," Eton said. "Nothing special."

"But, to a pro, they would lead them straight to Chico's apartment or his family's home in Sicily and then to us. But I still like to have my hands on any building blueprints, to help with my photographic memory," Cain said. As soon as all the paperwork had burned up, he turned toward Eton. "You ready?"

"Always," he said. "Let's go see who this Pedro is."

PETRA MIRKONOC STOOD at the edge of the airport with a sign in her hand, wondering how, once again, she'd been conned by her aunt into picking up strangers for the bed-and-breakfast. Ever since Airbnb had started, her aunt and uncle had the idea that they could make more money with a bed-and-breakfast than they did from her uncle's job. And they were right; they probably could. But it should be one of them standing at the airport with this sign right now, not Petra.

She didn't like picking up complete strangers, but thankfully this wasn't something she did normally. She would much rather be at the hospital in the labs, where she belonged. Instead, here she was, standing at the airport with a stupid sign. She studied the names: Cain and Eton.

They were very strange names to her. These were American visitors, but these didn't sound like any traditional American names she had ever heard of.

Just then the airport door opened, and a flood of people rushed out. She held up the sign and called out, "Cain and

Eton."

Nobody turned to look at her. She groaned. It was typical for her to have people who didn't realize they had a ride ready and waiting. Just as she was about to call out again, two men appeared, one on either side of her, almost pinning her in place. Not really, not intentionally, but they were so big that she felt hemmed in. Both stared at her with an intensity that had her gasping.

"Did you call for Cain and Eton?" the first man asked quietly.

She sucked in her breath, straightened, and said, "Yes. I'm from Pedro's B&B."

"Hi," he said. "I'm Cain. This is Eton."

"Hi," she said, feeling a little better. She opened the trunk of her car and put the sign inside. Then she turned and held out her hand. "I'm Petra."

Cain stopped and cocked his head. "It's your bed-and-breakfast?"

"No," she said. "My uncle is Pedro. I am Petra—with a *T*."

"Okay, good," he said. He motioned at the car. "Do you want us in the back seat or—"

"Anywhere you like," she said, with a smile. "Makes no difference to me. Anything to make you comfortable."

Cain took the front seat, while Eton slipped into the back, both opting to retain their bags. Cain noticed her eyebrows raised at that; so clearly she was observant. The car was a nice Audi, not something he would have expected a bed-and-breakfast to own. "Nice car," he said.

She looked at him briefly, then nodded and said, "It's mine. It doesn't belong to the bed-and-breakfast."

"Well, thanks for picking us up," he said.

It appeared that he was at least attempting to be friendly, but there was something about him. She couldn't put her finger on it—arrogance maybe. Just a sense of power around him that she didn't quite understand. She was forced to meet many strangers because of the bed-and-breakfast. It was one of the reasons she didn't hang around there more than necessary because she didn't enjoy the steady stream of unknown visitors. She enjoyed the privacy that came with her own place and not having to worry about others being there.

She didn't know whether she would feel better or worse about having these two men in the house. She told herself it depended on which side of the equation they sat on—figuring they were definitely people who had chosen a side. But she and her research work were all about the gray areas, thinking outside the box.

As she pulled into traffic, she said, "We'll be about fifteen minutes getting home."

"Do you live there too?"

"Oh no," she said. "I live in the village, but I'm doing this run for my aunt and uncle."

"Thank you again," he said, then fell silent.

But even his silence spoke volumes. She glanced in the rearview mirror to study the other man. He had the same hard look to him. She frowned, wondering just what was going on with them. "So, you guys here for a holiday?" she ventured.

"No," said the guy in the back seat, "mostly business."

She nodded but didn't quite know what to add. "What kind of business are you in?"

"Security," he added.

That made sense. They both looked well past the stage

of mere security guards, but maybe Secret Service or something like that. That power and sense of self-assurance again.
Their movements were like mountain lions on the hunt.

So that's what it was, she thought to herself. They were
intense. Like predators. She wasn't prey in this instance but
hoped to God she never found herself on the other end of
that intensity. "Interesting," she said. "That will be a first at
the bed-and-breakfast."

"What's the clientele normally like?" asked the guy sitting beside her.

Although he smiled, there was something uneasy about
it. She glanced at him nervously, then moved her gaze back
to the road. The traffic was on the mild side now, but it was
still almost noon, so it would grow busier getting through
the normal shopping and lunch hour. "Normally tourists
wanting to spend a week or so," she finally answered.

"*Hmm.*"

And again, nothing. She shook her head, checked both
ways, and darted through an intersection. "The roads can be
a little crazy," she admitted. "And the drivers are definitely
not the most mild-mannered, easy people around."

"Interesting," said the man behind her. "We're used to
crazy drivers though."

"Where are you from?"

"Lately the US."

"Oh," she said. "Your flight came from Switzerland, out
of Geneva though, right?"

"Yes."

Again he didn't elaborate. She frowned. "Well, you'll
like the breakfast offered at the B&B, and, after that, you can
get lunch and dinner from plenty of little places around the
village," she said. "A couple grocery stores are within walking

distance, if you just want a sandwich or something too."

"Good," he said. "Not sure how long we'll be staying."

"You've booked two rooms for two nights, haven't you?"

"Yes," he said.

She nodded and kept driving carefully through the area. People were well-known for jaywalking, as they crisscrossed the road, usually talking with their friends or with their arms full of fresh bread. She slowed her speed, as she watched several people step off the curb up ahead. But she was ready, and, before they ever made it partway through the street, she slowed down for them.

"I see that vehicles don't get much respect either," the guy up front said humorously.

"Small towns," she said, "people get distracted."

"And yet you stop, so that's good," the guy in the back said.

"What else would I do?" she asked in exasperation. "Hit them?"

"In the US, that might have happened," he said with a laugh.

That made her smile. "Not here," she said, as she pulled ahead, turned right, then left, and kept driving another seven blocks. Finally she pulled into a long driveway with access to the house at the back of the property. She pulled up to the front, which was a roundabout, then shut off the engine.

"This is our destination, gentlemen." She hopped out and opened the trunk. Both men had their bags with them, but she took out her sign with their names on it.

Just as she closed the trunk, the front door of the house opened, and her aunt and uncle came out. Immediately they came to meet their visitors. She looked at her father, who sat in a rocking chair on the veranda. She dashed up the steps and said, "Hey, Papa. How are you doing?"

As usual, she got the same vacant look and lack of response, which broke her heart. She bent down, kissed him gently on the cheek, and tenderly gripped his hand. "It's good to see you, Papa."

She heard the chatter of voices behind her, as her aunt and uncle greeted the visitors and ushered them inside. Petra sat on the front porch in a rocker beside her father. He'd been like this for the last year and a half. He'd had a car accident and had initially appeared to recover, but then he took a terrible turn, nearly dying, and hadn't emerged from this state of senility ever since. He ate, if the food was given to him, and drank, if a glass was put in his hand. Most of the time he would sit here and stare out at the scenery. If her uncle took her dad into the bathroom, he would go. If put into the shower, he would have a shower. But going from action to action was almost beyond him. It broke her heart to see him this way.

Her uncle looked after his physical needs; her aunt took care of his food and room. For Petra, well, she paid the bill. Sure, it was at a family rate, but somebody still had to come up with the money to keep her father. He had money of his own, but she hadn't even pursued using it, hoping he would recover and need it himself—or, as a fallback, someday he may need a higher level of care, and she'd need his money then. He was a relatively young man and could live quite a long time, though he didn't have much of a life at the moment. But Petra did what she could for him.

She also helped out her aunt and uncle whenever they needed it. Today was her day off, and, as soon as they found that out, they'd asked her to make the trip into town. It's not that she minded so much; it's just that going into the city was not what she wanted to do on her day off. With her free time, she pursued her personal medical research. Still, one didn't always get the luxury of choices. And who knew that better than she did.

A chatty voice called out to her. She shifted her gaze from her father to her aunt, calling her.

"Come in, Petra. Come in," she said. "You must come in."

Groaning, Petra stood.

CHAPTER 2

INSIDE THE KITCHEN, Petra walked over and put on the coffee. Her aunt seemed to think that, when Petra was here, she should play hostess, which was the last thing Petra wanted to do. She'd already been about as nice as she could possibly manage. Just something about these two new arrivals disturbed her in some way. Not necessarily in a bad way. In an unknown way. She shook her head. She would be very happy to take her leave sooner rather than later today.

Even the one who had spoken to her from the back seat had such a magnetic quality that it bothered her as much as the other one, who seemed more standoffish. They were both men she wouldn't want to see in a dark alley. But almost immediately her rational mind corrected her. *You don't want to see them in a dark alley—unless of course they were on your side. And God help anybody else who was in that alley.*

That's really what it was all about. It was just that sense of men who do right.

As she waited on the coffee, she opened up the breadbox, which her aunt always kept full of pound cake. Petra brought one out, sliced several pieces, and put them on a plate. Then she loaded up the cake and coffee on a serving platter and took it in to the two men. They sat there, in the front sitting room, having what passed for a social conversation, but they obviously made her aunt and uncle feel uncomfortable.

Taking pity on them, once she saw the beseeching look in her aunt's gaze, Petra sat down with her own cup of coffee. "These guys work in security," she announced. "They're just here for a couple days."

Almost instantly her uncle relaxed. Whether it was the fact that they were only here for a couple days, or that they were in security, Petra didn't know. "Are you working for a company then?"

The man who had sat in her front seat smiled. "More or less," he said. "We're just here to check out a few things."

Maybe not lies but definitely evasive, yet it came across smooth and completely in control and seemed quite normal for him. That made her a little more wary. She smiled at her aunt and uncle and said, "I already introduced myself. Did you two?"

Her uncle shook his head. "I'm Pedro," he said, reaching across to shake hands with the two men.

The quieter one said, "I'm Cain. This is Eton."

She already knew their names, of course, but she didn't know which one was which. Until now. Cain had been in her front seat, Eton in the back seat. Something about Cain and Eton was very strange to begin with, not to mention their names.

Her aunt smiled and said, "I'm Migi. Everybody calls me that."

Eton nodded and said, "The pound cake is really good."

Something was so honest and forthright about his tone that her aunt also relaxed. Petra wondered about that because it typically wasn't easy to get the two of them to calm down. Once they got upset about something, it took forever to settle them again.

Cain nodded, and both men looked at Petra, waiting for her expectantly.

She shrugged and said, "Now that we all know each other, I'll go spend a few minutes outside with my father, before I head home."

Her aunt jumped up nervously. "You should stay for dinner," she announced.

She stared at her aunt and frowned because the last time she'd stayed for dinner, her aunt had called her ungrateful. "I need to go home," she said in a calm, firm voice.

Migi shook her head. "No. Your father has not been well. He needs you to spend time with him."

"My father doesn't know if I'm even here or not," she said lightly. "As sad as that makes me feel," she said, "I know the truth of it, and I no longer feel guilty about leaving him behind."

"You still need to spend time with him," Migi said.

Petra rolled her eyes. She was trying to keep things polite in front of company, but it was a little hard when her aunt was pushing like this. "And why would I stay for dinner?" she countered.

"I'm making your favorite," her aunt said.

"And what's that?"

She named a traditional dish for their area, full of pasta, black olives, tomatoes, and fresh seafood. Petra could feel her resistance wavering.

Her uncle jumped in and said quietly, "Please, we'd love to have you stay. We don't see enough of you as it is."

He was trying to make amends for Migi again. Her aunt had a temper and often alienated people, long before they had a chance to get to know her. But Petra knew Migi very well, and she could be bitchy and mean. Petra laughed.

17

Cain looked at her and said, "It'd be nice to get to know you a little more," he said lightly.

She frowned at him. "Why?" she asked. "Unless you want to ask questions about the village, I don't know that there's anything we can really talk about."

"Fine," he said. "Questions about the village will be a good topic."

She felt like she'd somehow been maneuvered into a trap but didn't know how to explain it. She shrugged and said, "Fine, provided we're eating early."

"We'll be eating early enough," Migi said. She jumped up and headed to the kitchen.

Petra looked at Cain and frowned. "Why do I feel like that's exactly the ending you wanted?"

He raised an eyebrow, as he stared at her in a genial manner. "I'm not sure what you're talking about," he said. "I hope we didn't get off on the wrong foot somehow."

"No," she said. "I'm just tired."

Her uncle spoke up again. "She works hard," he said proudly. "She's a scientist."

"Doesn't matter what I am," she said, "because I'm not getting anywhere with my work anyway."

"What kind of work?" Eton asked.

"I'm doing research on dementia and Alzheimer cases, like my father has."

"Ah," he said, with understanding. "That's got to be difficult."

"Very," she said, "and it makes no sense."

"Bacterial?" Eton asked.

She looked at him in surprise. "I looked at that," she said, "but all the tests have come up negative."

"Maybe it's just a case of his body's worn out, and his

mind took an easy escape."

"And that could be," she said, "but it doesn't sound like my father."

"Sometimes the mind just takes over," Eton said. "And there's no real understanding of why."

"I've been in medicine for ten years," she said, with a sad smile. "Ten years. And since this happened to him in the last two, that has been my focus. There are just no answers."

Migi left the kitchen to rejoin them again. "So she quit," Migi said in an angry voice.

"No, I didn't quit. I just didn't find another avenue to pursue. I'm a lab technician. I work in a lab and have plenty to do," she said in exasperation. "I finance the research on my father on my own, but I have other work I must do."

"The lab should finance your father's case," her aunt said.

"Doesn't matter what they should or should not do," she said, almost by rote because she'd had this argument so many times. "They run a business. That means they must make a profit or otherwise won't have enough money to keep the bills paid. What I'm doing doesn't matter to anybody other than us."

"There are other people like your father," Migi snapped. And then she sat down heavily on the couch beside her husband. Her aunt was very pear-shaped, with an extrawide bottom and hips. The rest of her was quite small and tiny, but, when she sat, it was enough to make the couch shake. Her uncle looked at her, but he knew enough to keep quiet.

Petra got up slowly and said, "Well, I guess, if I'll stay for a little bit, I should go visit with him."

Her aunt opened her mouth to protest, but her uncle grabbed her hand and placed it on his lap. "She's fine. Let her spend some time with her father."

Migi forced a smile and nodded, as if to make everything sound like it was fine.

But Petra knew in her heart of hearts it wasn't, and, chances were, it never would be.

INTERESTING FAMILY DYNAMICS, Cain thought. They'd been shown their rooms and given an hour to relax before dinner was ready. Cain was grateful to have a hot meal right here the first night because it hadn't been a guarantee. The bed-and-breakfast typically only provided breakfast. The place was well-maintained but showing signs of aging. The fact that they were keeping Petra's father here and looking after him was also obviously a bit of a thorn in their side. He suspected that Petra paid them to do it, which was good of her, but the whole thing was probably very frustrating too. That she didn't stay here also said something about the family dynamics. Though, with that family sharing a house, it might be far too much to expect of her.

As he looked around his room, he noted the bathroom would be shared with Eton. Cain opened the connecting door and stepped through to see Eton hanging up his bag. "What do you think?"

"Seems like the family has some problems," Eton said thoughtfully. "And I'm sure the father's condition is a big part of it. Obviously the daughter is paying for his room and care."

"And yet there was no mention of it," Cain noted.

"No, but she's the one with a job, and the aunt and uncle obviously need the money. I think definitely some frustration and anxiety are there, maybe resentment over it all," Eton replied.

"Yeah, that was my take too," Cain said. "Don't know what happened to the father, but it's sad either way."

"Maybe nothing happened. We know he had a car accident, and clearly his brain is injured." He thought he knew what part of the brain was probably damaged. "Western medicine might have something to offer, but I highly doubt it. And Italy is well-known for their medicine and their advanced medical procedures as well," Eton said. "It's possible an ulcer or something is involved, but it's also possible that part of the brain just died."

"I don't think that's something anybody here wants to think about," Cain said.

"No, but, in the meantime, it looks like the daughter is keeping them all afloat. That's sad. Gotta be added stress for her."

"Yes, I wondered if Petra's funds are the only thing keeping the bed-and-breakfast running," said Cain.

"And yet I got the feeling it's been going on for a while."

"So maybe it's not terribly successful."

Eton looked around the bedrooms. "It's clean and neat, almost painfully so," he said. "But definitely older by twenty or thirty years. And I didn't see much commerce thriving as we came into town."

"No, and that's probably what the problem is," Cain said. "When you think about it, I'm not sure the uncle even works a job, and neither does the aunt. Looks like the bed-and-breakfast is their sole source of income. Petra is the only one who works, and as a scientist. I find that interesting."

"Interesting. Maybe it doesn't mean much."

"No, it doesn't seem to here. Still, let's see what we can find out about the family and about the town itself."

As they headed back down for dinner, things were a little lighter, as if the family had intentionally decided not to fight in front of strangers. Cain agreed with that, in theory, and hoped it loosened up their tongues because, right now, they could use some information.

As they sat down, Petra asked him, "So why this town?"

"Because it's obviously economically distressed," he said bluntly. That was just what he'd gleaned from the family's own turbulence.

Petra nodded. "Yes. We've been hit hard for the last few years."

"Do you know why?"

"We assumed it was just politics and annual seasonal spikes," she said. "But honestly the bed-and-breakfast hasn't been doing very well this year."

Migi immediately jumped up and said, "It's been doing just fine. It's been very busy."

As Cain looked back at Petra, she rolled her eyes. He hid his smile but understood the aunt and uncle were trying to maintain face, so they didn't lose more customers. But Petra was on the inside and knew things were definitely not the same as they had been.

"I think that's probably the course for the whole town, isn't it?" Eton asked.

"Several of the factories have closed down," the uncle spoke up. "That caused many of us to lose our jobs. I'm too old to get another one now, so we just live off the bed-and-breakfast."

"Good then," Eton said, "that we picked this place to stay."

The uncle smiled a great big beaming smile. "Maybe you'll come back too," he said. "Lots of the older families are here. I've had to make adjustments."

"Yeah? Like what kind of old families?"

"In this town there were four original families," he said. "They came in and started farming, gardening the orchards and the olive groves, and it just grew from there. The Marconis, the Rossellinis, the Roscos, and the Marshawns."

Marshawn was one of the names they were interested in. Cain glanced at his partner.

Eton nodded. "Are they all still running the land even now?"

"Yes," Pedro said, "but there hasn't been enough work for all the younger generations of the families to take over. That's been tough because some have gone off to do their own thing. But doing their own thing hasn't necessarily been easy or smart."

"And I guess it also depends," Cain said, "on whether those not-so-easy or smart choices have been good business decisions or not."

"Many of the young people have had to take on other jobs," the uncle said. "Some have gone into various business-es, like security and contract work. They travel all over the world."

"Slimeballs, if you ask me, the lot of them," Petra said.

"Chico, for one," her uncle said, nodding.

She grimaced at that. "*Ugh*. Chico's definitely a slime-ball. I understand nobody's even heard from him for a few weeks now."

"If he's such a slimeball, why does that worry you?" her aunt snapped.

"It doesn't worry me at all," she said. "I, for one, am not at all upset that he's not hanging around here."

Her uncle looked at her, surprised.

She shrugged. "You know how something about him gives me the creeps and always has."

"That's not fair," her aunt said. "Really, it's not. He wanted to go out with you. To take you to the school dances and such, but you would never give him even five minutes of your time."

"He's creepy," she said. "And he isn't someone I've ever wanted to spend time with."

"You didn't try," the aunt said. "You should have at least tried."

"No," Petra said, "I really shouldn't have."

Migi looked at the two men and apologized. "I'm sorry. This tends to be an ongoing issue."

"What, that she didn't date your choice in men?" Cain asked in a low voice.

"The man in question isn't somebody I would spend time with at all," Petra said. "In fact, I wouldn't be at all disappointed if he relocated permanently."

Cain looked at her with interest. She shrugged, but he wanted to know more. A lot more because that was one of the dead guys. He didn't want to tell her the man was dead though, because that would blow their cover. At the same time, he wanted to know about the rest of them. "Did he have brothers you liked better maybe?" Cain asked.

"He had two brothers," she said, "but one died quite a few years ago now."

"Under suspicious circumstances," the uncle said.

Cain looked at him. "What kind of circumstances?"

Immediately the aunt jumped up. "That's not fair," she said. "He was a good boy."

A story was here, and Cain was bound to get to the bottom of it, but it was Eton who asked, "So, was there a problem between the brothers?"

"And how," Petra said. "You have no idea. Those three used to fight all the time. But Barlow actually was a good man. I really liked him."

"But not Chico and not this other brother?"

"No. Tristan was slime too," she said. "Whereas Barlow would ask a girl out on a date, I heard Tristan was too much like Chico, who just assumed you would go out with him. He'd catch you somewhere, sit down, and take over whatever plans you had for the evening. There is nothing about him that I liked."

"Well, he's not here right now," her aunt said snippily. She got up, cleared away the plates from the table, and headed to the kitchen. Her uncle leaned over, patted Petra's hand, and said, "You know how she gets."

"Oh, I know," she said. "The trouble is, she just won't hear reason."

"What reasons?" Cain asked.

"Chico is scum—and he killed his brother Barlow, who was the only good one of those boys. But Chico killed him."

"On purpose?" Cain asked.

"Not according to him. And, according to the police, it was a bad accident. A bad accident where he ended up with a knife in the chest." She shook her head. "Sorry. I shouldn't get you involved in local politics," she said, "but Barlow was a good man. His father was the mayor at one time, and Barlow had similar political aspirations. Barlow was the eldest, then Tristan, and finally Chico, who is two years older than me."

"Interesting. I guess I pictured them as older than that," he said, as he thought back to the gunman. This would have put him maybe in his thirties, early thirties at that. It was

25

possible, but he'd thought the guy had an older look to him.

"If you'd seen him, you'd have thought that too. He lived hard, played hard, and looked hard. He'll come to a bad end one of these days. His father knows it, and I know he's already devastated. And given to drink. He hasn't recovered from the loss of his other son either because, in the back of his mind, he has always worried it was a deliberate killing."

"Sounds to me like it was," Eton said.

"It was," she said. "I saw it happen. I told the cops, but it didn't matter because it ended up being an accident by the end of the day."

"You saw it?" Cain asked. He looked at her and frowned.

She shrugged, got up hurriedly from her bench seat at the dining room table, and said, "Dessert time," as she headed into the kitchen.

Eton heard raised voices in the kitchen and then looked at Cain.

Cain shrugged and looked at him.

"It'll take a better man than me to go in there," Eton said.

Cain shouted with laughter, grabbed his glass of water, and headed straight for the kitchen. He heard the old woman, talking this time in a different language—the local dialect—and it flowed fast and hard. He had some knowledge of it, but it wasn't anything close to this version of it. Finally Migi saw him, and immediately the conversation stopped. He held up his glass and filled it from the sink. Once it was full, he turned and casually walked back to the table. The uncle looked almost a little dazed.

"So, if you lost your job at the factory," Cain said, "is there any other work around here?"

"No," the uncle said. "We lost hundreds of young families. It's really just all us old folks now."

"Interesting," he said. "We thought we might go for a walk around town after dinner."

"Go for it," the uncle said. "This used to be a beautiful place to live."

"I'm sure it still is," Cain said. "It's just different now."

The uncle looked at him, grateful in a sadly pathetic way, then nodded. "My great-grandfather used to live here," he said, motioning around the B&B. "I can't imagine that it was very easy in his time either. I try to keep that in mind all the time. Just in case."

"Just in case?"

"It doesn't matter," he said, with a smile. Then he got up, reached for his coffee cup, and headed toward the kitchen.

Cain and Eton shared a look, then stared at the doorway into the kitchen. Cain said, "That went well."

Eton shrugged his shoulders. "Can't say I feel like sticking around just now. Let's head out," he said.

The two men stood, and Eton called out, "Thanks for dinner."

As Cain got to the front door and went to close it behind him, he saw Petra, standing there in the hallway, hands on her hips, staring at him, an odd look in her eye. He smiled and closed the door firmly between them.

CHAPTER 3

PETRA HEARD SOMETHING that Cain had said as he walked out the door. It had been a very awkward dinner, but the questions from the strangers seemed more pointed than anything. But then she was supersensitive on the subject. As she stepped out on the front porch to have coffee with her father, she held a plate of dinner for him, so she could feed him. She watched the two men as they strolled down the street, stopping to look at various buildings.

She couldn't imagine what their conversation was about now or what interest this old town could hold for them. And she highly doubted any businesses here were of interest to them. She patted her father's knee and turned his head, so he looked at her, and said, "Dinner, Dad." She held up the fork, and, using her other hand, she opened his mouth and put the fork in. As soon as she did that, he chewed.

When he was done, he opened his mouth, and she filled it again and again. It had been like this since not long after he'd come home after the accident. The doctor seemed baffled by it, saying that her father was stuck between progress and this weird decline he was in. He was present; yet he wasn't. By the time the plate was empty, he settled back to rock gently in place.

"At least you seem happy enough," she said.

He didn't speak; he didn't utter a sound anymore. She spent a few very relaxing minutes enjoying her coffee, then kissed her dad goodbye and got up, taking the dirty dishes inside. Quickly she rinsed them and loaded them into the dishwasher. As soon as she was done, she headed out, picking up her purse and sweater.

She called back to her aunt and uncle, "I'm leaving." Not waiting for a reply, she walked down the steps and across the sidewalk to her car. She hopped in, turned the vehicle around, and headed to her home. Several blocks down the road in the same direction, she saw the men walking. One of them turned to see her coming up behind them, and she lifted a hand as she drove past.

Taking the next corner in front of them, she turned left, and then took the next right, driving past the corner property, where she shook her head sadly. It was Petra's former family home, a place her aunt and uncle had struggled with because it was bigger and nicer than theirs. It had belonged to Petra's father, but she had lived there too and, should her sister ever come home, was meant to be a home for her as well. But no more. With a shake of her head, she continued on another block and pulled up outside her apartment.

She didn't know what it would take to get her sister back here anyway.

Getting out of her car, Petra grabbed her purse and her sweater and headed to her door. Her neighbor's dog greeted her. Chico often waited for her to come home so he could get extra cuddles. After sharing a big hug and a kiss, she walked over and checked to make sure the dog had food and fresh water on his porch.

"You've got both. Now it's my turn. I'm going inside and getting food and a hot cup of tea." She gave him an extra cuddle then walked inside her place. Next she put on the teakettle and opened the back door, so she could sit outside with her tea.

"It was a crazy day and a crazy evening," she muttered to herself. Going through everything she had in the cupboards, she pulled out a cookie from a package, and, with a fresh cup of tea, walked outside to the backyard.

She sat for a long moment, enjoying the sunshine. When she heard a "Hello," she immediately recognized the voice and knew it was Cain, the one who sat in the front passenger seat in her car on the ride from the airport.

"Hello," she called back.

Cain and Eton appeared in her backyard. Cain explained, "We have a few questions."

"Why ask me?" she asked. "What information could I possibly have for you?"

"Well, I guess it depends on your relationship with the family. But we wanted to take a look at the house you were telling us about. The big fancy one, whose father lost the one son and has two others, but one was missing."

She laughed. "Missing? Is that what you call it?" she said. "That no-good son of a bitch probably ran off."

"You feel rather strongly about that. Why?" Cain asked.

"Because he more or less ruined my sister before he left," she said tiredly. "Well, he or his brother Tristan anyway. Both of them for all I know. But she got pregnant, possibly had an abortion, which got ugly between us. She was acting pretty irresponsibly and was always a little standoffish afterward. One day I came home to find she'd packed up and left. There was a note, saying she needed time. She just took off, and I haven't seen her since."

"Ouch," he said. Eton nodded solemnly. "How long ago

was that?"

"About eighteen months, I think," she said. "It's hard to pin it down. It was around the same time as my father's accident. I wondered if it all didn't happen at the same time."

"Meaning?"

"When he had the accident, there was no reason for him to be driving. There was no reason for him to be out anywhere, unless he was taking my sister somewhere," she said. "So I've always wondered about it."

"That would be tough," he said, "losing them both at the same time. I'm sorry. That just makes it even worse."

"No need for it to be worse," she said, fatigue heavy in her voice. "As you can tell, it's not a great scenario at my aunt and uncle's either."

"No," he said. "It sounds like everybody's having a rough go of it."

"Absolutely," she said. "It is what it is, but I don't understand why you're so interested in all this." She looked from Cain, who was doing all the talking, to Eton, who remained silent this whole time but fully aware.

"Because it's an oddity," Cain said cheerfully. "Just blatant curiosity really. Chalk it up to ignorant Americans."

She laughed. "I highly doubt that," she said. "I don't think you do anything without good reason."

He looked at her in surprise.

She shook her head. "No, don't look at me like that," she said. "You guys are guys on a mission."

At that, they both stopped and studied her. "And why do you say that?"

"You're not tourists," she said. "Not even part-time. You obviously came here for a reason, but I just haven't figured out what it is yet."

Cain gave her a half smile and said, "Well, maybe we'll check out the father's house, and we'll see for ourselves."

She hesitated, then said, "I'll come with you." She walked down the front pathway, opened the small gate, and let herself out.

"Is there a reason why you'd join us?"

"Because his father has always been a crazy-ass son of a bitch," she said. "After losing the one son, he got even worse. Drinking more and more."

"Of course," Cain said, "but how crazy?"

"Gun-shooting crazy," she said briefly. "And, if he doesn't know who you are, he'll probably shoot you without asking questions."

"Nice town," Cain said.

She looked at him, shook her head, and said, "No, it's not. Not at all."

"Why do you stay?"

She shot him a hard look. "So that my sister has someone to come home to. Besides, I can't just walk away from my father."

"You'd make better money elsewhere."

"No doubt," she said, "I would. And I'll get there one day. But, in the meantime, my father is like a living ghost, and my sister has left home for God-knows-where. The only family I have left are my aunt and uncle."

"And they'd be lost, if you didn't continue to pay for your father's care."

"Exactly," she said. "So I'm kind of stuck, just waiting for somebody to crack open this stalemate that my life has become."

"Careful what you wish for," Cain muttered. "Sometimes what we think we want isn't really so, and we don't figure that out until after the fact."

She looked at him, gave a hard laugh, and said, "What I can tell you is that something has been going on in this town for a long time, and that means I'm a big part of it, whether I want to be or not."

He stared at her for a moment, gave a clipped nod, and said, "Good. I want to see him then."

She shook her head at him, in shock. "Didn't you just hear me?"

"Oh, I heard you," he said, "but it could be exactly what we're looking for."

I SHOULDN'T HAVE said that much, really, Cain thought to himself. But, as she led the way at a clipped pace, he found himself falling in line beside her, Eton trailing closely behind. "Are you always this edgy?"

She shook her head. "No, just today, I think," she said, visibly trying to relax.

He reached out, picked up her arm, hooked it through his, and said, "We're just out for a nice friendly stroll," he said. "Come on. Relax."

She looked at him in surprise, stared down at their linked arms, and shrugged. "This won't get me relaxed. No way, no how."

"Why not?"

"Because we're going to his place, Morgan's place," she said. "Something about that man I don't like."

"All the better to hang on to me then," he said quietly. "So what's the deal?"

"Like father, like sons."

"Did one of them ever hurt you?"

She shook her head. "Not badly," she corrected. "A couple times I thought it would get uglier with Chico, but he just stuck to name calling and threats."

"Fear is a wonderful deterrent. Did he have a job?"

"Yeah. Anything anybody would pay him for," she snapped. Then she took a slow, calming breath. "Like I said, he's just bad news."

"I'm sorry."

"Me too," she said. "I thought I was getting over it. But it seems like just the mention of his name is enough to set me off." She looked up at him. "So, now that you found out what we know about him, will you be leaving town?"

He gave her a look.

"Well, I can see that you're not here for anything else but that family, so let's figure out what you need to know, and then, at least, you can get on with your life. Unlike the rest of us."

"What if I told you that he was dead? Chico, I mean."

"I'd probably laugh and cry and maybe shout with joy," she said bluntly. She stopped and looked up at him, searching his gaze.

He shouldn't have mentioned anything about that either.

"Well? Is he?"

"Possibly," he said. "We think so, but we're still waiting for a positive ID."

She fell into step once more, and they moved forward again.

Cain glanced at Eton, who just shrugged. There was no real way to understand or to know the best way forward at this point.

"It'll break his father's heart, if he's dead," she said.

"Because of the loss of the other one?"

"No. Because Morgan would probably want to kill Chico himself," she said, with a bitter laugh. "The father used to be a mercenary in the military," she said. "So, if you're planning on going up there, be prepared. He's also crazy with grief and anger. Plus drunk."

"You think he figures this one, Chico, killed the other boy, Barlow, like you said?"

"Absolutely. I told him flat-out what happened. But then he bought off the police, so that Chico at least had a clean record. That's kind of Morgan's thing. He said he didn't want anybody else to know about it, and I'd better shut up or else."

"Or else?" Cain asked softly.

She looked up at him, smiled, and said, "Welcome to the backwoods of Sicily."

Cain nodded, his gaze distant. "Well, let's hope it doesn't come to that. I'd love to ask him some questions though."

"Like?"

"*When did you see your son last?*"

"I told you, not for a long time," Petra said.

He looked at her sideways.

She frowned. "Okay, fine, I think he's been back-and-forth. I just don't know when. He and his father get along sometimes. Last I heard, his father was upset that he stole some weapons."

"And are weapons such an open topic around town?"

"No." She groaned. "Chico has a sister, and she's a friend of mine. But her father keeps her on a short chain."

"Sounds like that might not be a bad thing, considering

the brothers," he said.

"Well, she's about to bust out," Petra said. "She wants to go to Rome. Her father will lose another child."

"Maybe it's because of the way he is."

"And those loser brothers," she said. "So we'd have a better chance of talking to her than Morgan."

"Lead the way," Cain said. "I need answers."

"To what kind of questions?"

"Who was paying the Chico kid to do his latest job?" he said bluntly.

"Why?" she asked, stopping and standing in the middle of the street, her gaze going from one man to the other.

"Because we think he killed a friend of ours and badly hurt two others," he said.

She wrinkled up her face at that. "Are you planning on killing him when you find him? The father, I mean?" she asked in exasperation.

"No, not unless he gives us a reason."

"You should know that this town will close ranks," she said. "If there's any ugliness, you can't expect any help from the law or the locals."

"No," he said. "I can't say I particularly expected otherwise."

"It's always been that way here," she said quietly. "Even if they do something wrong. It's like the town protecting bad pennies, especially the wealthy and dangerous ones, and the rest of the world can stay out."

"Understood," he said. "What I would really like to do is get access to Chico's apartment and take a look inside."

"Well, he does keep an apartment in town here, but he's never there," she said. "What? Did you not know that already?"

"Yeah, but we also know he went to his father's place all the time," Eton said.

She turned and slowly started walking down the street again. "That's right. He did. And it would be just like him to have an apartment, then not use it."

"Why is that?" Cain asked.

"Because he's a sneaky son of a bitch," she said with a frown.

"Listen. Don't tell anybody that Chico's dead, okay?" Eton said.

"Hell no," she said, "that would just get me in trouble. Better off if you guys deal with that yourselves."

"Exactly," Cain said with a smile.

They turned several more corners, and, although it was late summer, a gloominess hung in the evening. She looked up and said, "You must have brought this weather with you," she said, "because it was a beautiful sunny day earlier."

"Clouds are good," Cain said. "Too much sunshine's not good for the soul."

Petra burst out laughing. "Then I wonder if there'll ever be sunshine in my life again," she said.

This time when he glanced at her, he saw a look of sadness that broke his heart. He grabbed her arm again, not exactly sure why he felt the need to touch her, and said, "Come on. Let's go take a look."

As they got close to the property, he noted the massive wall surrounding it all.

"Stone walls?" Eton said.

"Very Italian," Cain stated.

Pulling out her phone, she made a call.

"Who you calling?" Cain asked.

"Patina," she said. "Checking to see if she's inside."

Just then a vehicle pulled out the driveway. It stopped just at the street's edge, and a woman, sitting behind the wheel, answered her phone. When she realized Petra was calling her and that her friend stood right there, Patina rolled down the window. "What's up?"

"Where are you going?" Petra asked, looking down at her friend.

"I'm leaving," she said. "My dad is in a real temper, and I've had enough. I'm out of here for good. I'll call you later."

"Do you want to tell me about it now?"

The young woman shook her head sadly. "Nothing to tell. He's just really losing it, and he's dangerous as hell. I'm done." With that, she rolled up the window and pulled away.

Surprised at the turn of events, Cain turned to look at Petra and asked, "Now what?"

CHAPTER 4

"I 'M NOT EXACTLY sure," Petra said, "because, if Morgan's in a temper, the firearms will be close at hand."

Just then a shot rang out, and it hit the stone wall at the gate. A man yelled, "You get the hell off my property."

She answered him in Sicilian. But he roared at her in English.

"Does he always speak in English?"

"Ninety percent of the time," she said, frowning at the house. "Your daughter just left," she called out.

"She can stay away too," he shouted back.

"Why is that?" Petra asked.

"She's no daughter of mine." Again more shots were fired.

She brushed the hair off her face. "Dammit," she said, shaking her head. "When he gets like this, he's just impossible."

The man came storming out, and she sighed, as they witnessed a big, tall old man carrying a long shotgun.

Eton and Cain shared a frown.

She smiled up at the old man. "Patina just left. Is this how you treated her?"

"It doesn't matter how I treated her," he rambled, then took several steps and stumbled.

He was obviously in a drunken stupor.

She sighed and said quietly to Cain and Eton, "It's better if we don't talk to him right now."

Morgan took several more steps and tripped. He hit his head on the concrete in front of them and laid completely still. She gasped. She wanted to rush to his side, but Cain grabbed her arm. "Wait. He's still dangerous."

She looked down at Morgan on the ground and said, "Outside of that gun, which he's not even holding now, he's nothing. He's not dangerous. He's just a sick old man." She raced to his side. The two men followed. She studied Morgan. "He's out cold. While he's unconscious, go ahead inside through the front doors, bear to the right, and you'll find a hallway. Take the stairs. The last bedroom on the right is Chico's."

"Are you sure?"

"Go now," she said, "while Morgan won't know the difference."

CAIN, NOT WASTING a moment, dashed inside, Eton with him. Neither wasted time on the drunk, who had stumbled and fallen on the pavement. They followed Petra's directions to the bedroom at the end of the hall. Cain didn't even want to know how she knew which bedroom was Chico's, but, given Petra was friends with the sister, maybe it made sense after all. The door was locked. He stared at it and then faced Eton. "You think it's rigged?"

"No," Eton said. "Presumably there's still some love for the family here."

"I don't know about that," he said. "Seems to me not a whole lot of love is lost on any of them."

Eton already had his pick out, quickly popped the lock,

and, as they pushed it, found a deadbolt. Eton noted, "You know that this means he had to leave from inside the room." That deadbolt took a little bit longer.

"I know, maybe out the window or some secret interior staircase," Cain said, but the minute they opened the door, the smell hit them. Immediately pulling his shirt over his nose, he stopped and stared. "What the hell?"

On the bed was a woman. Or at least what remained of a woman. She'd obviously been dead for quite some time. Cain looked back at Eton. "Let's hope this isn't Petra's sister."

Eton's gaze widened at the thought. He nodded with a hard clip and said, "But we need to do something about this."

"I know."

They pulled gloves from their pockets—the thin surgical disposable kind that they carried everywhere. Avoiding the body as much as they could, they searched for a very obvious cause of death and found it—a bullet through the forehead. They walked on the carpet, trying to leave as little sign of their presence as possible. The fact that they'd found a body would give them a little bit of an excuse to be here but not too much more. They opened the nearby closet, and Cain whistled. It contained nothing but heavy artillery. "This is a hell of a weapons stash," he said.

"Kind of makes you wonder how long it's been here."

"Probably a hell of a long time," Cain muttered. Staying out of the way of the window, they made sure nobody else would know they were here. They made a quick check through the closet, closing it up the way they had found it in the first place, noting it was there in case they needed some weapons themselves. Then Cain checked a night table, finding a small black journaling book, which he pulled out and tucked into his pocket. Also he found a stash of cash in a bag, which he left as is. He took one last look at the woman on the bed and motioned for Eton to go ahead of him. As they exited the bedroom, he stopped and looked at the lock. The two turned toward each other. Cain shrugged and said, "We'll leave it open." And, with that, they swept down the stairs.

Just as they opened the front door, a bullet slammed into the doorjamb at their heads. Eton grabbed Cain, and they both fell backward. Cain looked through the window to see Petra flat on the ground outside, beside the old man. Cain called out in a low voice, "Petra, did you get hit?"

She shook her head slightly.

He had to get her into the house or at least farther away from here. When he went to swing open the door again, another shot was fired. He pulled out his phone and sent a message back to the team, giving them an update.

We need cops, he typed, **and a dead woman's in the upstairs bedroom.** At that, he got back a simple message.

On it.

Looking around at their options, Cain caught sight of a big metal lounge chair off to the side, with a thick padded seat. With the door wide open, he dashed outside, grabbed the lounge chair as a protective covering, and raced to Petra's side. He pulled her to her feet, and together they inched their way back, holding the chair up as a shield. Several bullets struck the metal and bounced off harmlessly or were embedded in the cushions. Back up on the porch, he pulled her into the house. "What about the old man?" he asked, putting down the lounge chair inside.

"He's still out cold," she said, gasping for breath.

He faced her. "Did you see the shooter?"

"No."

Just then they heard sirens far off in the distance. Nearby, a vehicle suddenly started up, and, as they watched, a big black truck drove from the neighbor's property, around the stone wall, and took off in front of them. Cain couldn't see the driver; the truck was too far away. He looked at Eton and said, "We need that tracked."

Eton was already on his phone, texting off their request.

Cain quietly asked Petra, "What does your sister look like?"

She glanced at him in surprise. "Red hair, about five feet, seven inches, very slim."

He looked at her, took a deep breath, and said, "I need to show you something, but it's pretty unpleasant."

She frowned at him and said, "If it has something to do with my sister, I need to know what you're talking about."

He looked at Eton, who gave a one-arm shrug. What else could they say? "A dead woman is upstairs," Cain said.

She stared at him in shock and shook her head. "No, it can't be her. She left months ago."

"Months and months ago, or months ago?"

She frowned. "She left at the same time my father had his accident. So it's been eighteen months."

"Any idea when the Chico guy living here would have disappeared?"

She shrugged. "I'm not sure. He came and went all the time."

"Well, before the cops get here, do you want to take a look?"

Her face paled, but she nodded grimly.

"If nothing else," he said, "you could identify her,

whether your sister or not." He led the way upstairs and into the bedroom.

A few seconds later, Petra timidly stepped around the corner, reacting to the smell. When her gaze landed on the bed, she cried out, her hand slapping across her mouth.

Taking a step toward her, Cain wrapped his arm around her shoulders and asked, "Is it her?"

Tears poured out of her eyes, as she looked up and nodded.

"I'm so sorry," he said, then motioning to the door, he escorted her back outside and closed the door.

"She's been here all this time?" she asked, her voice little more than a whisper.

"Yes, it looks that way," he said. "A sealant was put around the door and the windows, probably hoping to curb the smell, but also so the body would dehydrate and mummify versus decompose."

"I know it's hot here but still—"

"The flies already found it, and that was a long time ago," he said. "So her body has decomposed some already."

She shuddered at his words, but the sight of her sister was worse.

He just hoped she hadn't noticed the incredible mass of worms and maggots in various stages on the bed.

"How could there even be anything left of her after all this time?"

"Depends on how many months she has been here. The forensic specialists will have to figure all that out," he said.

She gave a bitter laugh. "Small town. This won't be very pretty."

"Maybe not," he said. "But it doesn't mean that it shouldn't be dealt with." He paused, frowning at Petra.

"Didn't you say something about a baby?"

She nodded. "Well, there was a pregnancy. Did it end in a baby? No, maybe not," she said slowly. "I'm not exactly sure what the end result of that was." Still obviously in shock, she just stared up at him. "For these last few months at least, she's been right there," she said. "That's just crazy."

"I know," he said. "But nothing to be done about it now. Nothing more to be done for her, except to get justice."

She stared at him. "This is—it's just too unbelievable."

"I'm sorry, Petra," he said. "That's the reality we have to deal with."

She gazed at the scene out the front door. Then her focus landed on the old man, still outside on the ground. "Did he know?" Her voice was louder and angrier, as if she'd found a target responsible for the atrocity done to her family.

"I don't know," he said. "That's something we may get some answers to, once he is conscious and sober. But honestly it'll be a bit of a mess when the cops get here, which won't be long from the sounds of it."

She shot him a hard look and dashed out the front door.

CHAPTER 5

P ETRA BENT OVER the old man on the ground and started ripping into him. She flipped him onto his back, partially mindful of his head wound, but, at the same time, desperately in need of answers. She gave him a hard shake, and, when he groaned, she spoke loudly. "Morgan, wake up!" she snapped. "I need answers." His eyes fluttered open, and he glared at her. She snapped back. "A dead woman is in your house."

But it didn't seem to filter through the fog in his eyes. Yet he finally reacted when he saw Cain, standing behind her. The old man's eyes widened in fear. She looked back and saw Cain standing there, like an avenging angel, his hands on his hips, glaring down at the old man.

"Who is he?" Morgan asked in his native language.

She answered in the same. "He's here looking for your son."

"My son is gone," he said, tears coming to his eyes.

"No, not Barlow. Chico," she said impatiently. "Chico."

"A bad seed."

"Well, that bad seed has been hiding my sister in his bedroom," she said, her voice hard. "She's dead." He stared at her, and she saw the truth in his eyes. "You knew!" she gasped. "You knew and did nothing?"

He just closed his eyes and sagged back.

Cain reached out and placed a hand on her shoulder. "Didn't you say he started drinking really heavily a few months ago?"

She looked at Morgan and then back at Cain. "You think he found out then?"

"I think he found out but didn't know what to do about it. He said his son Chico took off, and he obviously wasn't planning on coming back, if that's what was here waiting for him."

"Dear God," she whispered, sitting back on her heels, her hands over her eyes. "This is the one time I'm glad my father won't know or understand what's going on."

"I'm so sorry," Cain said.

The sounds of the sirens grew closer.

She stood up slowly and looked at Cain. "I just … I just—" She stopped, completely at a loss for words.

He smiled, nodded, and opened his arms. She walked into them and burrowed against his chest. "To know that she was right here in recent months. I thought she was somewhere across Europe. I wondered about the baby, but I didn't know and had no way to find out."

"I didn't see any evidence of a child," he said, "so maybe that's a good thing."

"It's definitely a good thing," she murmured. "But now I feel like I should go back up there and make sure there isn't a dead child."

"You know there won't be a live one," he said, "and, if there's a dead one, we'll find out when the forensics team and the cops get here."

She just shuddered and nodded. "They won't like you having gone into the bedroom."

"Maybe not," he said. "We'll just say that this guy said

something to justify our actions."

She thought about it for a moment, then nodded. "Let me talk to the police first."

"The trouble with that is, we won't know what you said, so what we say later could contradict you," he warned. "You'll need to keep it simple."

"Okay," she muttered.

When the cops arrived, she quickly explained what had happened. They took one look at her, at the old man on the ground, and at both Cain and Eton, then raced into the house. She knew that would be the focus from now on. It wouldn't matter what Morgan had done. Not the shooting today or the heavy drinking he'd kept up steadily, because all Morgan wanted to do now was drink some more, so he wouldn't have to deal with the next few months.

As it was, an ambulance arrived and checked him out, but he refused transport to the hospital to get any care for his head injury. He didn't say very much of anything. Once they got him upright, he just sat on the porch steps and stared into space, with almost the same blank look that her father had.

Petra sat down beside him, speaking in their native language. "You knew all this time," she said. "You knew how much my family had suffered."

He didn't say anything.

"But you also suffered," she said, trying to find a way to understand him, to find some way to make sense of him just leaving her sister here. "It didn't bother you at all that she was rotting a few feet away from you?"

He didn't say a word.

"Instead, you just sealed up the room tight and left it. My God," she said. "Did you kill her yourself, or did your son do it?"

He shifted uneasily at that.

"You know the cops will have questions for you," she said. "No way they can shield you from it this time. This is way too big," she said. "You can't just fire your gun to scare them away. Not to mention the fact that another shooter was trying to kill the three of us. While you were out cold on the sidewalk, somebody from the other side of that wall over there tried to kill us."

He looked at her with a sharp gaze at that point, and she realized he really was in there and listening.

She nodded. "Were they after your son Chico?"

He got an odd look in his eyes, but he shrugged. "I don't know," he said. "He's a bad seed."

"Do you know who Chico was working for?" she asked.

"Tristan."

She looked at Cain and shrugged. "He says Chico was working for Tristan."

"Ask for any details that you can get."

Knowing they probably didn't have much time, she quickly turned back and said, "Please tell me. What kind of work was he doing for Tristan?"

"Devil's work."

"Killing people?"

He just shrugged.

"Theft, drugs, burglary, anything? What was it?"

"All of it," he replied.

She sagged back with a big sigh. "Right, a bad seed."

Morgan nodded slowly.

"And Tristan? Do you know where they would meet?"

"No," he said. "But all that was before Chico left, before Tristan left."

"Do you know where Tristan is now?"

"No," he said, shaking his head.

"Do you know how they kept in contact with each other?"

"Phone."

Petra looked at Cain and asked, "Did you get Chico's phone? Apparently Chico and Tristan communicated by phone."

Cain frowned at that, pulled out his own phone and sent a quick text.

She looked back at the father, not nearly so imposing now. "He's dead, you know." The old man looked at her in surprise. "Your son, Chico," she said. "He's dead." But instead of the sorrow she expected to see, there was what looked like relief. She thought about that for a moment. "He's caused you a lot of trouble, didn't he?"

The old man slowly nodded.

"Did he threaten to kill you?"

He nodded even slower.

"And, if you were to say anything about my sister, he'd put a bullet in your head too, right?"

He nodded again, even slower.

She groaned. "Well, I still wish you would have said something, but Chico's dead, and he can't hurt you anymore. He can't hurt anyone."

The tired old man just stared out into the horizon.

"Was he your son?"

"I don't see how," he said. "Bad seed."

She looked up at Cain and shrugged.

CAIN ENCOURAGED HER to continue with her questions.

"What's the deal with Tristan?" Petra asked Morgan, but the old drunk man just shrugged. "Who does he work for? Do you know company names or anything at all?"

She kept asking questions, now in English for Cain's benefit, but the man had sunk into some drunken haze. It made sense now that he'd been drinking so heavily. But no way that dead body would remain undetected forever. Possibly until he died. Maybe the son—whether Chico or Tristan—would come back and take care of Morgan and torch the place. It was an incredibly sad scenario. Maybe Tristan still would resort to arson.

Cain looked back at the house, as he listened, and he realized how large the wing on that side of the house was. Cain looked at her and said, "I want to go back inside and look at the floor below Chico's bedroom."

She nodded. "The cops are inside. They may not let you."

"Well, I'll give it a try," he said.

With Eton at his side, the two of them walked in, slipped past the cops, and headed directly to the rooms under the wing where the body was found. He couldn't believe there wouldn't be some kind of decomposition impacting the floor below. But the climate was so dry here, and, with the room sealed up like that, he didn't know. As they headed to the room downstairs, he exchanged a look with his partner.

"Do you think something's here?" Eton asked.

"It's time to find out," Cain said. Reaching forward with his gloved hand, he checked the knob. It was locked. He quickly popped the lock and pushed it open.

They stood in the open doorway, surveying the scene. The smell was strong down here, but nowhere near as bad as upstairs. Some people might not have known the difference. The room was completely empty, except for a series of large cupboards. They walked through to them and pulled open the doors, but nothing was here.

He looked behind the cupboards, wondering why these were even here. "I wonder if this was an office or something. He could have come up and down the stairs, and no one would have noticed anyone was working down here."

"An office for what though?" Eton said. "Everything's gone."

"It wouldn't take much to clean it out." He motioned to a tiny piece of something white stuck behind a particular cupboard. Even with the two strong men, they had to put their backs into it in order to shift the big sturdy cupboard. After moving it, Eton reached down and pulled out a photo.

It was the gunman, Chico, from the museum, with someone else. The other man was slightly older and had a hand on Chico's shoulder. They looked like they could have been related.

They both studied it, wondering where the picture was taken. It could have been anywhere in Europe. Cain flipped it over and saw the name Tristan written there. "Okay," he said and immediately took a photo and sent it off.

"It'd be nice if we could get more on this Tristan guy," Eton said. "And find out what he was into."

They worked together to move the other cupboard slightly too. Behind it, they found a series of envelopes taped to the back.

"I wonder how long ago he did this," Cain said. Hearing footsteps and voices on the stairs, he said, "We need to hurry."

They quickly ripped everything off the back of the wardrobe cupboards and, along with the photo of Tristan, put it all together, and slipped out the side door, the police none the wiser. Walking around the front, they went to where Petra sat beside the old man.

Cain held out the photo to the old man. "Is this Chico?" they asked, pointing to the one from the museum.

He looked up at it and nodded.

"And Tristan?"

He nodded.

"They got along?"

He nodded and shrugged.

She quickly started to ask him questions. And this time he spoke in his native language.

"They get along to a degree. Tristan is dominant and uses Chico," she said, looking at the photos. "Tristan is older, so I didn't go to school with him and don't know that much about him."

"Good enough," he said. "Do you need to stay here?"

She sighed. "Most likely." She looked up at him. "Are you leaving?"

"We found some stuff we want to sort through," he said quietly.

She nodded. "Go on back to the bed-and-breakfast. I'll come down in a little bit."

With that, the two men turned, slipped through a side gate in the stone wall, and walked back to the bed-and-breakfast. Cain knew the cops would probably come after them pretty quick, looking for statements if nothing else, and he and Eton would be happy to provide them. The bottom line was that it was a pretty shitty time frame right now for added complications. Their first focus was on finding Bullard.

Cain and Eton walked through the front door to the bed-and-breakfast and headed straight to their rooms. They saw no sign of the older couple, which was a good thing, although Petra's father still sat outside on the front porch. Upstairs in their rooms, they quickly opened up the envelopes and took photos of everything, sending it to their team. Then they sat down to diagnose what the hell they had found.

"This looks like a hit list," Eton said of the piece of paper in his hand. "And Bullard's name is on it."

Immediately Cain rose, took one look, and whistled. "Well, this is the best connection we've found yet. So it appears Chico was essentially working for this Tristan guy? Acting at his bidding anyway. And what is Tristan's deal? Is he the one who's been hired out to take down Bullard's team, or is he the one doing the hiring?" Remembering the little black book he'd stashed in his pocket, he pulled it out, skimming over its contents fast. Cain said, "I'm not sure if these are contacts, but there are names, dates, and places."

"We'll have to analyze all the content," Eton said, holding out his hand.

Cain passed it over. "Money is listed too. So I'm worried that the list is a kill sheet."

"In which case, it's a good thing that Chico asshole is dead," Eton muttered. He went through some of the names on the list, reading out a couple of them.

Cain didn't recognize any of the names. He was busy working on the piece of paper in his hand that had Bullard's name on it. He sent that off to his team, knowing that everybody would be working on it, including Ryland. As soon as Cain sent it, his phone buzzed with replies and answers from the rest of the team. But Cain wanted to make sure they all had copies of everything.

He sat down and placed one particular envelope on the bed and carefully went through it. It was a machinery list. Weapons that Chico had; weapons that he liked; weapons he would buy again. It was almost like a shopping list of what to get. Then Cain noted the tiny little marks on the side of some guns listed here, and he remembered seeing a couple of those in the closet.

"Looks like this is a list of his weapons cache," Cain said, laying down the sheet of paper. "Most of this was not easily obtainable."

"Somebody's got contacts," Eton replied. "Tristan maybe."

"Apparently. I'm still frustrated as hell though." He looked at the list that had Bullard's name on it. The thing was, Bullard's name was in the middle. "I wonder if this is a wishful-thinking dead list," he muttered out loud. "And did you notice that nothing is checked off?"

"Right. So it's almost like a possible assassination list," Eton said.

"Regardless we're not on it," Cain said. "That's weird."

"No, but see that little mark beside Bullard's name? I think it's a plus sign, maybe signifying the team."

"That could be," Cain agreed. "What we need to do is figure out if everybody on this list above Bullard's name has been taken out already."

"And we've got to focus on finding this Tristan guy. He's the connection we have to work with now."

"Hopefully the team can take that old photo and find out what he looks like currently. We really need a new photo," he said.

"And we need it, like, now," Eton agreed.

"Might be a little easier said than done." He looked at Eton. "I wonder if our hosts here know anything about Tristan."

"Go ask," Eton said. "Everything that we've got here basically connects all of them, and, with Bullard's name right there in black-and-white, we know it's related to him. But it's a matter of who Tristan is connected to that would hire him for something like this. Unless he's the one doing the hiring, but then the question would be *why*." Both of their phones buzzed just then. Cain looked at the message and said, "The name on the top of the list is dead, taken out eighteen months ago."

"So it is a kill list," Eton said.

"They'll work their way down," he said. "And there are three names after Bullard. Just because our guy Chico died, that doesn't mean Tristan or one of his thugs isn't still after them. And us too for that matter."

"Who do you want to contact?"

The two men looked at each other. At the same moment, they said, "Ice."

"I'll go talk to Petra's aunt and uncle downstairs," Cain said, heading to the door, with the photo of Chico and Tristan. "Check to make sure Ice has all this and bring her up to speed."

"Will do."

When Cain walked downstairs to the kitchen, he found the old couple sitting at the kitchen table, talking over a cup of tea. As soon as he walked in, silence fell. They hopped to their feet. "Do you need something?"

He shrugged and said, "Sit down for a moment. Do you know these men?" he asked, as he held out the photo.

Immediately Migi's face twisted with distaste. "This one

we spoke of earlier," she said, pointing to the dead gunman Chico. "But this one is definitely trouble."

"Who is he?" Cain kept his tone neutral, as he leaned back against the counter.

She shook her head. "We don't talk about such things."

"Which only adds to the mystery," he countered.

The uncle looked at his wife, then back at Cain. "Tristan is Chico's older brother. When they were young, Tristan was the local ruffian, breaking into all the houses. He would slash tires and kill cats," he said, shaking his head. "When he disappeared, we all breathed a sigh of relief. But then he came back as a man. He carried guns and knives and was bad news."

Migi shrugged and said, "This one, he picked up the local boys and turned them bad too."

"More than just the one? Chico?"

"Tristan turned the local thugs and troublemakers into true criminals."

"And how would we find Tristan?"

"You don't," she snapped, getting quite cranky about the whole thing. She wrapped her arms around her chest and said, "Stay away from him. He's bad news." And, at that, she turned her back, effectively ending the conversation.

Cain reached over, picked up the photo, and said, "Well, I guess I have to find him my way then."

Immediately she turned and cried out in alarm, "You can't."

"Why not?"

"You'll bring him back to this town. We don't want him here," she said, her stress evident.

He slowed down. "Is he that bad?"

She nodded. "He would shoot you as soon as look at

you."

"A lot of men are like that in the world," he said, his voice hard.

The old man looked at him, a tremor evident in his hands and his lips as he spoke. "Please, if you contact him, leave our home."

"Do you think he'll come after you?"

"Yes, of course he will," Pedro said. "No one is safe if he is around. They're both bad, two peas in a pod really, but Tristan? He's the worst."

And, with that, Migi got up and left the room.

The old man slowly stood. "She called the cops on Tristan once, way back when," he said. "He was bad news back then, but he's really ugly now. He's always threatened to come back to take her out. So she steers clear of him."

"What would be his reason to go after her?"

"She called the cops on him," he said. "The same reason he killed cats as a teenager. Just because he can."

Cain nodded slowly. "Got it," he said. "At the same time, it might just give him a reason to come back and have a second chance."

"He doesn't need a reason. He would do it just for fun," the old man said. "Please don't bring him here."

At that, Cain said, "In that case," he said, "we'll find another place to stay."

"That's probably a good idea," he said. "We don't need this kind of trouble."

"The trouble was here long before we came," he said. "It always has been."

"That's true, but now you are stirring up stuff that will hurt Migi."

"Did she ever do anything to hurt him?"

"Except for calling the cops, no," he said, "but even that was too much for this asshole."

"Well, we'll see about it in the morning." And he walked back upstairs.

He knew that, from somewhere inside the house, Migi was watching him. He didn't know where, but the layout was such that there were likely little hiding spots for her to check out her guests because she was just that kind of person. But it was obvious that she was legitimately spooked. Now he wondered if anybody would get any sleep in this house tonight.

As he walked back into their rooms, he heard Eton on the phone with Ice. By the time the call was over, Ice was totally up to speed. Unfortunately she also didn't have any good news on Bullard. Cain bit down his disappointment on that. His team was out searching. Her team was out searching. For all he knew an entire army had been mobilized. Since Terkel had confirmed that Bullard was still alive, then Ice would dive under every wave to find him.

Terkel was rarely wrong. Still everyone had to be wrong sometime. Maybe this was the time. But Cain sure as hell hoped not.

Just then Eton said, "Some weird undercurrents are going on in this town."

"They're really spooked downstairs," Cain said. "They've asked us to leave, if we contact Tristan. They're afraid of a certain amount of retaliation."

Eton looked at him in surprise. "For what?"

Cain quickly explained what Tristan was like growing up and how Migi had called the cops on him.

"And he still threatens her?" Eton asked.

"What they saw when he was a teenager was a total disregard for life, torturing animals and such. And, when he came back years later as a man, he mobilized all the younger toughs into his own little gangsters."

"Well, we don't have to stay here and make them uncomfortable. We can gather all the information we can get tonight and will pull out early tomorrow."

"That's what I was thinking," Cain said. "They'll be happy enough to see us go." He looked around at the paperwork. "You learn anything new?"

"Nope," he said. "Not so far. Strange that Petra isn't here yet."

Cain stopped at that. "She should be back by now, shouldn't she?"

"Except for the fact that she doesn't live here," Eton reminded him. "She did say she was coming back though," he added quietly.

"I know. So I'm wondering what the holdup is." Cain thought about that and said, "I'll go back and take a look."

CHAPTER 6

"**Y**OU THINK THAT'S wise?" Eton asked Cain.

"Maybe not, but I don't feel like I can leave her to deal with all this alone. And we don't know who that shooter was after." The more he thought about it, the darker his soul felt. "I don't like anything about this now," he said. "I'm gone."

With that, he raced from the bed-and-breakfast and headed back to the crime scene. What he really wanted to know was if she was okay. But, in his heart, he realized things were not only *not* okay but that something seriously wrong was going on.

PETRA HAD BEEN sitting on the step beside the old man, as the cops came and went. Several came to talk to her a number of times.

They'd asked her about the two men; she told them to go to the bed-and-breakfast. One had already been dispatched in that direction. She just shrugged, knowing the men could hold their own. The fact of the matter was that, if they hadn't gone into that bedroom, her sister still wouldn't have been found. She just couldn't believe her sister had been lying here dead for all this time, for months. They didn't even know how long yet.

The cops had asked her several questions about it, and she was hard-pressed to come up with actual dates when she'd last heard from her sister. But then even that was blurred. When was the last time she heard from her via phone? She didn't know. And, no, she had no idea what happened to the child. Her sister had threatened to keep it and then, in the next breath, had threatened to abort it.

Petra never did get any answers, but to think of her sister lying up there with a bullet in her forehead, having been there for several months, was just beyond anything she could comprehend. And to know that this old man beside her had known. She just shook her head and buried her face in her hands.

When she heard the whispered words from beside her, she finally came out of it and stared at Morgan in shock. "You're sorry?" she asked in confounded disbelief. "You've let somebody lie there in that condition for God-only-knows how long."

"Four months," he said. "Four months and twelve days."

That was the first inkling she had as to how much it had cost him too. She groaned. "And you seriously couldn't tell anyone?"

He shook his head. "Chico told me what he'd do to me."

"And it's quite possible he would have carried out his threats," she said, "but he's gone now."

"Good," he said sadly. "He should never have been born."

"Maybe not, but that doesn't mean that what you did was any better."

"I didn't kill her," the old man said. "And those two men you came with? They're the same."

"Are they?" she asked dubiously. "I don't think so."

"They are," he said. He looked at her. "Don't end up like your sister."

She winced at that. "I wasn't planning on it." She couldn't find anything inside her heart that said these two men brought out the same feelings as his son's interest in Petra used to. "They may be in a similar industry," she said, "but I think they're on the side of the good guys."

"The side of the good guys changes," Morgan said, with the wisdom of somebody who'd lived long and hard.

"Is that what happened to you?"

He nodded slowly. "And then I wanted out. I wanted to retire. I wanted to have my family. Only to find my family was worse," he said sadly.

"I'm sorry about Barlow," she said.

"Chico killed him," he said. "Chico killed him deliberately. There was no need for that. Barlow was a good boy."

She nodded. "There was no need to kill my sister either," she said gently. "Did you talk to her when she was here?"

He shook his head. "I didn't know," he said. "I didn't know. But the boy told me there was something in his room that I didn't want to see. He said I wasn't allowed to open the door, and, if I did, he'd know. When the shots were fired at you today, I figured it was Chico."

"How would anybody know?"

"The door was triggered," he said, "to send an alarm to somebody. I guess to the neighbor. And whoever it was, was supposed to kill whoever opened the door."

"Well, they didn't get us," she said quietly.

He gave a broken laugh. "They're not done, you know? They're never done, people like that. He's just biding his time, waiting to come back around again."

She winced at that and then looked up at the street. The cops came and asked her more questions. She answered as honestly as she could, but there wasn't anything to say. When they got to why the men wanted to look into the room, she said they'd had past dealings with Chico and were trying to track him down. The cops just nodded. That family was very familiar to those at the police station.

"A lot of weapons are up there." The cop looked at the old man. "We're taking them."

The old man looked at him and nodded. "I don't care," he said. "But if you take them all, you leave us defenseless."

"These weapons are not for household use," he said, "and, if you have a license, you can have your own."

"I do," he said.

She snorted at that. "He shot at us as we came up the sidewalk."

The old man glared at her. "I didn't want visitors."

"We'll be taking that gun too," the cop said.

She watched as weapon after weapon was carried out of the house. When something really big was carried out, she whistled silently. "Is that like a rocket launcher or something?"

"Or something," the old man said.

"Are these all new? Like, in working condition?"

He nodded. "Like I said, bad seed."

"When was the last time you talked to my sister?"

"I didn't talk to her at all," he said, "because I stayed to my side of the house. They came and went at all hours."

"Did you see her?"

"Not really," he said. "There were always women. Your sister was just one of many."

"She'd hate that," Petra said.

"Of course, but she still came."

"Of course," she murmured. Just then she watched as a tall man strode down the street toward them.

"Interesting. He's coming back," she said.

The old man looked in that direction. "He's dangerous. Watch yourself." After that, he went silent.

She asked Morgan a few more questions, but he wasn't interested in answering. When Cain walked up the front steps to where she sat, he asked, "Are the cops still on it?"

"Yes, they just hauled out an arsenal of weapons."

"Good," he said. "Some very high-end pieces were in that lot."

"Surprised you didn't take them for yourself," she challenged.

"I have no need of them," he said.

"This guy here," she said, motioning at the old man, "said the door was triggered to send a signal to somebody when it was opened."

Cain raised an eyebrow, thought about it, and said, "And that would explain the shooter."

"In what way does that explain the shooter?" she said in exasperation.

"He wasn't a good shot," he said quietly. "I suspect he's been living next door, and, now that the door alarm has been triggered, he's long gone. Probably been here so long that he forgot to take his shit with him."

The old man looked at him and started to laugh. "You're right there," he said. Only he said it in such a broken language that Cain wasn't exactly sure what he'd said. Petra quickly translated.

He looked at the neighbor's place and asked Morgan, "You know who it was?"

The old man looked at her, she translated, and he shrugged. "Another bad seed."

"So do you think anybody'll care if I go take a look inside that house?"

The old man looked at him, shook his head, and said, "You probably should. But it might be triggered to blow."

"Great," Cain said under his breath. Then aloud, he said, "You'd better stay here then, Petra." He turned, and, rather than going to the front sidewalk and walking around the stone wall, he headed to the hedge.

Before she realized it, he'd already slipped through. "Smooth," she said admiringly.

The old man glared at her.

She shrugged and explained how easily he'd gotten through the hedge.

"I told you that they're the same," he said.

Just then the gurney came down, carrying the body of her sister. She jumped to her feet, her hand to her lips, as she stepped back to give them room. It was just so painful to see her like this. She'd been so vibrant and alive. And what she was now was not even dead. It was like she was rotting from the inside out. And that was just so wrong.

The coroner gave Petra a sad look, as he walked beside the gurney to the ambulance. She knew he couldn't tell her much that she didn't already know. Her sister had been shot. But the cops didn't know whose hand to place around that gun. She had a damn good idea, but the asshole was dead already.

She looked at the cops as they came out, and she asked, "Can I go home now?"

He nodded. "We know where to find you."

"And what about the other two men?"

"We'll talk to them tomorrow morning," he said. "We've got your statement right now, and we'll get theirs when we talk to them first thing."

She nodded and turned, heading down the sidewalk. As she turned to leave, the old man called out, "Watch your back."

She stopped and thought about that, then turned and smiled at him. "Thank you." As she got to the sidewalk, she turned right toward the empty neighbor's house, after Cain. As she got around the side of the stone wall, she noted that this house was almost as dilapidated as the main house next door. Much smaller and older, probably once a part of a grand estate, now sold off piecemeal, just a rental.

She walked to the front steps and knocked. Cops were all around, and they had checked out the place, but, with the shooter's truck long since gone, nobody seemed to care.

Cain answered the door, and he held it open for her. "Come on in."

"Is anybody here?"

"Not now," he said. "I would ask if you knew who rented it."

She shook her head. "I don't come down here very often," she said. "This is the ratty part of town. Nobody does."

"Understood," he said. "The thing is, somebody's been living here. It'd be nice to know who."

"Well, track that truck," she said. "That'll tell you."

"There's got to be a real estate rental database somewhere too," he said.

"Maybe, but, on the other hand, I don't think anybody really gives a shit. We have a lot of empty houses where people move in and squat," she said.

"Good to know," he said. "And something to keep in

71

mind."

She nodded, walked slowly around the house, and asked, "Did you see anything useful?"

Yes," he said. "Come here. I'll show you." He led the way into the bedroom.

There she stopped at the doorway, not sure what she was looking at.

"Looks like he might have been trying to pack in a hurry, but, when he ran out and left, he probably took off with just the one bag and obviously left this one behind."

She walked over and peered inside. "What is it?"

"Electronics," he said, with a nod of satisfaction. "Which also means he'll be coming back in the dark to get it."

"And?" But she knew the answer ahead of time. "You want to stay here and wait for him, don't you?"

He gave her a note of satisfaction, with a clipped nod. "I sure do," he said. "It's a perfect opportunity to find out exactly what the hell's going on."

She looked at him. "I want to be here too."

"NO WAY," CAIN said calmly.

"Why not?" Petra asked.

"You're not prepared," he said. "This is a fight that you can't win alone."

"He was shooting at me."

"He was shooting at anybody and everybody," he said. "Chances are, he'll come in with a gun, trying to sneak in and out and be gone. He'll leave town and possibly the country even."

"How long do you think he's been here?"

"Well, if you had any kind of security images," he said,

"we could check, but, as it is, I suspect since Chico left."

"Of course," she said. "He was just here to keep an eye on the house, wasn't he?"

Cain nodded.

"And that's why he can't afford to leave this stuff behind. Have you gone through it?"

"I still have to do that," he said, "but I got the laptop up and running." He pointed to the desk on the side.

"Wow." Then she nodded. "You're right. He'll come back for this—and quick." She thought about it for a moment. "He can't drive the truck," she said. "So he'll have to walk in on foot."

"It could be a cop," he said. "Did you think about that?"

"Maybe, but why would it be?"

"Depends on if they're getting paid," he said.

She thought about the people who might have lived down here. "My aunt and uncle will probably know."

"Maybe call them and see," he said. "I'm definitely not their favorite person anymore."

She pulled out her phone and walked off a few paces and called her aunt. A rapid-fire conversation followed that he couldn't do anything more than stand here and listen to.

When she hung up, she said, "A cop was living here. Just a young rookie."

"Well, guess what? That young rookie is in this up to his neck." His voice was cheerful, upbeat.

She frowned at him. "Why are you so damn happy about it? It's a bad cop."

"But it also means," he said, "we have a good chance of catching him." Just then Cain heard the faintest of noises outside, still a way off and moving slowly, trying to not make noises like Cain just heard. Cain grabbed her and pulled her close. "I want you to go back home," he whispered. "It's too dangerous for you."

"Like hell," she said, but lowering her voice too. "I'm in the middle of this, whether I like it or not."

"No," he said, "not yet you aren't. And, if we can keep you out of it, we can keep you safe."

"Have you forgotten that I was also shot at and that he would have recognized me?" she asked. "Do you think that, once you're gone, this will be over?"

"I hope so," he said, looking down at her. "The last thing I want to do is to leave you here as a target."

"I'm a target already," she said. "So, until we solve this, I'd just as soon stick close."

He stepped back slightly.

"I mean it," she said. "You can't just push me away."

"Well, you're not giving me a chance to," he said, with a half laugh.

She shook her head. "No. And I won't. Like I said, it's too important. I live here."

"Would you live anywhere else?"

"In a heartbeat," she said. "I'm just not sure what to do about my father."

"He's not unhappy here, is he?"

"No, but I'm not sure he's getting the best care."

"I'm not either actually," he said, thinking about it. "But I'm sure you have old folk's homes here that would do better for him."

"Yes, but I don't know if he would be happy there either."

"I'm not sure anybody's happy anywhere sometimes," he said, with a sad smile.

She shrugged. "You know what I mean."

"I do."

She stopped and looked at him. "Why do you even care anyway?"

"Why do I care about what?"

"If I ever wanted to leave?"

"Just wondering," he said, but something odd was in his voice.

She glared at him. "Are you thinking, after this is all over, that I won't be welcome here?"

"I have no idea," he said honestly. In fact, he'd been thinking out of his own curiosity because there was just something about her. "I don't want to lose track of you."

She shrugged. "You're not making sense."

"That's a common problem," he said, laughing softly. He reached out and gently flicked her chin. "But remember. I can't have you making a sound here."

"You think he's coming?"

"He's already here," he said, with a half smile.

She froze.

He held a finger against her lips and said, "Remember. Not a word." And he moved them both into a nearby hiding space.

And, sure enough, she heard a noise. As she waited right behind Cain, she heard the sound of more chaos outside.

"Why is he making so much noise?" she whispered.

An odd buzz came on his phone. He pulled her close and whispered, "That's the signal."

"Signal for what?" she whispered back.

"We have company."

Just then the back door burst open, and a man dressed in all black came striding through. He walked right past where they hid in the hallway—among all the boxes and the shadows everywhere—so it wasn't surprising that he didn't see them. He headed straight into his bedroom, then snatched up the bag without thinking, and raced back toward the door. He never made a sound.

As he reached the door, Eton filled the frame instead. The cop froze and said, "Just who the fuck are you?"

"Well, I would say, your worst nightmare," Eton said, with that humorous voice of his. "But he's actually behind you."

The guy spun around to look, just as Cain reached out with his right fist and plowed it into his jawbone. There was a delightful sound of bone cracking, as the man went down. When Cain heard Petra gasp beside him, he looked at her horrified face. "We need answers," he said, with a shrug.

She nodded, her fingers clutched together. "But that sound. God, it was awful."

"He'll be fine," he said.

Eton picked him up under the ribs and dragged him into the kitchen, where they sat him down and tied him up.

"What will you do with him?" she said.

"We won't hurt him any more than we have to, but I need to know about this Tristan guy."

She said, "Right. Because you so badly wanted to learn about who hired Chico."

"Right. He killed a good friend of ours, hurt two others on our team," Cain said absentmindedly. He turned and looked at her. "And we're all on his hit list too."

She shook her head furiously. "He's trying to kill you?"

Cain nodded. "And Eton and the rest of our team," he said. "We'd like to stop him before he succeeds."

She gulped and nodded.

Just then the man in the chair started to wake up. He

groaned, then lifted his hand, only to find it restrained. He came awake with a hard snap. "What the hell? Who are you?" he asked, struggling against his ties. "What do you want?"

"Good, you speak English," Cain said. "But then you're not from around here, are you?"

He glared at him. "I'm a cop," he said. "What are you after?"

"Well, if you're a cop," he said, "you're just one more of a million bad cops, so I care about justice."

"I'm not a bad cop," he said. "I haven't done anything wrong." But fear was heavy in his tone.

"Except for the fact that you shot at me," she said in outrage.

He looked at her and said, "And who are you?"

"My sister's been dead in that house for months," she snapped. "I would like to know what your part in all this was."

His eyes widened. "What are you talking about?" he said. "I didn't have anything to do with a dead woman."

"Oh, so you don't know that the house you were guarding hid a dead body? The same house with the alarm that went off, notifying you to take anybody out who was there? Which was exactly what you tried."

The younger man's face blanched, and his eyes filled with terror. "No, no, no," he said, "I was paid to look after the house."

"And yet you shot at us," she said in outrage.

He looked at her. "Just to scare you."

"No, that's not quite true," Cain said, "or you wouldn't have shot at the doorjamb, where we were standing."

The man's gaze narrowed. "There was a bonus, if I took

out anybody inside the house."

"And that is exactly what we want to know," Eton said, slowly moving closer. "Who would pay that bonus?"

The cop hesitated.

Petra interjected, "Tristan, right?"

Cain reached across, grabbed her hand, and pulled her up close. "We've got this."

She glared at him and then realized that was his way of telling her that she had screwed up. By supplying the name, it was possible their dirty cop would just latch on to that, instead of giving them the true name.

But the guy looked at her and said, "He'll kill you even for mentioning his name. You know that."

"Does that mean he'll kill you too?" Cain asked.

"Does he know that you left all the electronics behind?" Petra asked.

The questions came hard and fast. But the kid just kept shaking his head. Finally he yelled out, "You don't know what Tristan's like. He'd kill all of us right now, if he thought we were talking about him."

"He can try," Cain said, and, just as he spoke, a single shot was fired through the still-open back door. And just like that, the young cop's head exploded.

CHAPTER 7

PETRA WAS PICKED up roughly and dragged out of sight.
"Oh, my God. Oh, my God," she kept whispering against his chest, as Cain held her tight. "Tristan's out there, isn't he?"

"Yep. The kid probably told him that he had to come back to the house. And, by doing that, he opened it up for somebody else to find all the electronics. That's a mistake that's hard to walk away from."

"So that means that we're now in the line of fire."

"Oh, we definitely are," he said. At that, he looked around, but Eton had already slipped out of the front door. "But this is what we do, so don't worry about it."

"Don't worry about it?" she said, shaking her head. "That's hardly something I can do."

"No, not yet," he said, "but Eton's gone out after him." They heard the sound of a heavy-duty vehicle ripping down the road. "But not with him taking off," he said. "Damn."

"How did you know Tristan would be here?"

"I figured the guard and Tristan would both show up," he said. "We did set up a camera down on the far side of the street, when we were looking for license plates."

She shook her head at him, stunned. "This is an insane world you live in."

"It is," he said. "But, even worse, they're all gunning

after me and my team. So we'll do anything we can to protect ourselves."

His voice was hard, and she had absolutely no doubt that he meant every word he said. She looked down at the dead kid and sighed. "Guess that means you'll have to call the cops back."

"Yep," he said. "We will." And, with that, he untied the man.

"They'll want to talk to you and will probably throw you in jail for this," she said.

He glanced at her and smiled. "Not likely. We have friends in high places. Except for the blip on the radar locally for having a bad cop in their batch, it won't be deemed much, as far as the police are concerned."

"Is that even fair?" she said. "I don't even know who you are."

He looked at her, gave her a half smile, and said, "You know what matters."

"No, I don't," she said. "I really don't."

He leaned over, kissed her gently, and said, "Yes, you do. We look after the good guys."

"Says you. But how does anybody even know who they are here in this town?"

He gently traced her lips and whispered, "Sometimes things have to happen in a certain way."

She struggled with that. But when she heard another vehicle pull into the long driveway, she frowned. "Your friends?"

"Yes," he said. And, sure enough, a group of men arrived. Conversation was short and brief, and she never got to see any of their faces. He grabbed her arm gently and led her to the front door. "It's better if we're not here."

"Jesus," she said, reaching up with a trembling hand.

"It goes on all around you," he said. "The trick is to be with the good guys."

"That line between the good guys and the bad guys," she whispered, "it's getting mighty thin."

He wrapped an arm around her, held her close, and whispered, "Not that thin, I promise. Now, can I walk you home?"

She nodded slowly. "Are you going back to the bed-and-breakfast?"

"I don't think your aunt and uncle want us anywhere near there at this point," he said.

"Well, my place isn't fabulous, but you're welcome to a couch," she said.

Eton joined them just then. "I'm good. I'll head back to the B&B," he said. "You go with her and make sure she's safe." And, with that, the three parted.

"What did he mean by that?" she asked.

"Part of this cop's job—of guarding the house—would have been to send photos to Tristan," he said. "Almost everybody would have wanted photos. It's one of the reasons I really wanted to see those electronics."

"And was he sending photos?"

"He was transmitting, from bugs inside the house. And out. So, the photos were being sent, but we don't know who was receiving them."

"Will this team be able to find out?"

"Yes," he said. "Or that's the hope anyway."

"Jesus." They walked in silence. "I don't know if you should be staying with me tonight."

"Why?" he asked. "Are you worried about being alone with me?"

"They would have seen both me and you at Morgan's house. So chances are, we'll still be under attack."

"Which is why I'm coming," he said. "I want to make sure that you're not alone."

"It's not so much about being alone," she said sadly. "It's just—nobody's ever safe, are they?"

"In many ways, no," he said. "So you have to go about your day, hoping that you're one of the 99 percent of the population who has nothing to do with this kind of life."

"Right." She shook her head. "What got you into this business?"

"I went into the military to serve," he said. "After so many years, I'd had enough of all the rules and regulations. I had a good friend who was working for Bullard, so I joined his team. So, you know what they call a mercenary?"

She frowned at that. "I don't think that's a very nice word."

"I'm definitely not a mercenary," he said. "I am, however, a security specialist." As they walked toward her apartment, he said, "And I sure don't see any security in this place at all."

She shrugged. "It's a small town. Nothing ever happens here."

"Yeah? How do you feel about that now?" he asked, with a half laugh.

"I feel like nothing will ever be the same again," she said quietly. She motioned at the front door and said, "Come on in. Nothing fancy."

They went inside, and, when she opened the door, he asked, "Was it even locked?"

"Yes," she said, "but it's not much of a lock."

He walked in, did a quick search of the space. "Looks

like the place could use more than a better lock."

"Not while I'm paying my aunt and uncle to look after my father," she said sadly. "I don't make a ton of money doing what I do. Any extra money I have, I've been putting into research on my father's condition."

"Any luck with that?"

"No," she said. "But we don't have the facilities or the grant money for the type of work that really needs to be done."

"I'm sorry about that," he whispered.

"It's a form of dementia," she said. "I just don't know what form it is."

"That can make it tough too."

"Indeed," she said. "But it is what it is." She motioned to the bedroom. "I have spare blankets for you," she said and disappeared into her bedroom. She snagged two blankets and a pillow for him and returned. She dropped them on the couch.

"So, that house you pointed out earlier, that was your family home?"

"Yeah. Though I'm just as glad it's gone. It's always been a sore subject to Aunt Migi. My whole life, she was offended because it was bigger and better than her own, in her eyes. And this apartment is what I can reasonably afford right now. You would probably be more comfortable at the bed-and-breakfast, where you'd have a real bed."

He looked at her and said, "But you'll sleep better if I'm here."

She looked at him in surprise, then shrugged. "Yes, it's been a disturbing evening." She stopped in the middle of the room. Not sure what to do.

"Go. Get ready for bed," he said, his voice soothing and

gentle. "I'll be fine here." He sat down on the couch and tested it.

She laughed, wiping at her eyes. "It's not built for somebody your size."

"Furniture is rarely built for anyone my size." He looked up at her. "Go on to bed. Do you have to work tomorrow?"

"No," she said, "I'm not working for a couple more days." After that she headed into the bathroom—the only one in her apartment. It had two doors, so guests could access it via the hallway, but she could privately enter it from her bedroom. She felt weird locking the one door now, sharing her bathroom with a man. Shaking her head at that thought, she quickly brushed her teeth and washed her face. When she was in her pajamas, she unlocked the hall door, went back into her bedroom, where she called out to him from behind her bedroom door, "The bathroom is all yours."

She went into her bedroom, closed the door, curled up in her bed, and closed her eyes. She wondered how one would turn off all the nastiness she had seen today. It was one thing to be shot at by an old drunk, but it was quite another to be shot at because she was at Morgan's house and his bad-seed sons had set some sort of an alarm. But then to find her sister there and to know that she'd been there for months, it was really just too much.

She didn't even know if she could cry or grieve; it was such a shock still. And maybe that was a better way to put it. Maybe it was best that she couldn't yet because it was just so much. It was hard to find any kind of closure, when there were no answers. Having no answers really didn't help. She frowned as she waited for sleep to claim her.

She heard Cain moving around the apartment, but it all seemed to be so quiet and so simple out there. How did he live in a world so chaotic, while the rest of them were just barely hanging on? It seemed like there were no answers for anybody. And it seemed that way because it was that way. He was right; just go about your day, and hope nothing was going on in your space that would bring you into something like this. A scary thought but definitely something to keep in mind. Finally she closed her eyes, and, after several long heavy sighs, she drifted off to sleep.

OUT IN THE living room Cain could almost tell when Petra drifted off to sleep. It was almost as if a sense of peacefulness came from her bedroom. It was disturbing to see just how in sync they were because she didn't seem to have the same sense about it that he did. Or she simply wasn't in tune with it enough to realize they had a connection. She would probably put it all down to the craziness in her world right now. And, to a certain extent, she would be right.

But there was more to it than that, and he couldn't keep himself from asking if she would ever leave the area. He couldn't see himself staying in a place like this. And, after all was said and done, he doubted anybody would want them around. Not long-term.

Her father, on the other hand, was another issue entirely. Cain could really appreciate the fact that she had looked after him, even trying to do research geared for him. That alone might be enough to keep her heading in another direction, so she could do more research. He didn't know though. She seemed to be pretty stuck on staying close to him.

Cain was stretched out, as best he could on the couch, wondering how he would get through the night without kinking his back, when Eton called from the B&B. When he answered his phone, Cain asked, "What's up?"

"We've got the ambulance here," he said, his voice calm and steady.

"What happened?" Cain asked, as he bolted to his feet.

"The father, he appears to have passed away."

"What? Just like that?"

"Yeah. Just like that. Apparently that can happen, but what do I know? The only death in my world tends to be violent."

"Jesus, she just got to sleep."

"There's nothing she can do," he said, "but she probably won't appreciate it if you don't wake her up."

"Yet what can she do?" He knew she wouldn't like it but decided not to tell her right away. "Are they taking him to the hospital?"

"Yes," he said. "She'll see him tomorrow morning most likely."

"For a chance to say goodbye, you mean? Yeah. What about the aunt and uncle?"

"They're pretty upset, lots of tears and a lot of— caterwauling, I would say. But I have to wonder if they really cared or if it's mostly about the steady income."

"That must be the brutally honest outlook we've gained from our constant exposure to the seedier side of life," he said, "because I had the same thought. Sad, isn't it?"

"Well, it's pretty hard to make a living here, and, although they may have hated it, that is the reality that has kept them going."

"And there was obviously some bad blood between the branches of this family. So it's hard to say what they'll do now." Cain sighed. "I think I'll leave it be for now," he said. "I'll tell her in the morning."

"If she's not already been wakened by somebody contacting her," Eton warned.

"True enough, but let's see if we can get her at least a few hours of sleep." And, with that, he hung up.

He just couldn't imagine what this would do to her, especially knowing how focused she was on trying to find a cure for him. She'd been through a lot already, and tonight had to have been terribly hard for somebody who didn't have any exposure to the type of violence that Cain lived with on a regular basis. It's not that he wanted to, but somebody had to because, as far as he saw, a world full of bad guys always meant there was a world full of honorable men, who wanted to do something good to help out. Trouble was, there always seemed to be more assholes than the good guys, and that just sucked. He sat up and pulled his phone toward him and sent off emails, looking for more answers.

There had to be something somewhere. When one of the teams contacted him and said the dead cop at the house was another of Tristan's young buddies, they said they had a line on finding Tristan.

He sent back a text. **Where? When? I need a time and a place, and I'll be there.**

When we figure it out, we'll let you know.

Their subsequent reply came, and, even in a text, the words sounded short. He hit the Talk button and called his team member this time. "We need this solved," he said. "Another woman is involved now too. And her father's dead, although we think it's probably of natural causes."

"What is it with you guys?" Fallon asked. "How the hell do you keep finding women in the middle of all this stuff?"

"It's not that we're finding women," Cain said. "The women are already here."

"Says you," he retorted, with a note of humor. "Because it just seems like you're constantly finding trouble for yourself."

"Maybe so," he said, "but I'd like to keep this one alive if possible."

"Is she special?"

He hesitated and then said honestly, "Yeah, she is."

"Interesting," Fallon said. "What is this? First Ryland and then you?"

"Hell no," he said. "Just because I want to keep her safe and to let you know that she's special doesn't mean it's a done deal."

"No, it probably isn't a done deal," he said. "As a matter of fact, why would it be? Shit's going on in her world, and she's got to blame you for some of it."

When they hung up, Cain wondered about that because that would be a crap deal if it were true. But a lot of common sense was behind Fallon's comment, and that made Cain feel even worse. He hoped she didn't blame him for the trouble, but, if she did, he'd have to spend some time convincing her otherwise.

CHAPTER 8

P ETRA WOKE UP groggy and disoriented. She was in her own bed, in her own bedroom, but it seemed like nothing else was hers anymore. As if the life she had been living had changed in some fundamental way, and she wouldn't recognize anything. Feeling odd and unsettled, she lay under the blankets, wondering at the chill that had settled inside. It was summer and was supposed to be hot here and definitely warm, even at this early hour of the day.

She checked the clock beside her and confirmed it wasn't even six o'clock in the morning yet. But something just felt off.

Slowly she swung her feet to the floor and, pushing the blankets back, got up and walked to the window to look outside. The events of the night came rushing back. The fights, the gunfire, the shooter, the man in the house beside them and—her sister.

She bowed her head, willing the tears and the grief to come pouring forward, but everything was still locked behind a stone wall, where her sister had stayed all that time she was supposedly gone. It drove Petra crazy to think that her sister had been here for the last few months and hadn't even stopped in to say hi. What kind of family member did that?

But she immediately answered it herself. A family member who wanted nothing to do with her family. Petra headed to the bathroom and turned on the shower. She quickly tossed off her simple nightshirt and stepped under the hot spray.

It was hard to imagine ever being clean after a day like she'd had yesterday. She worked in the sterile world of test tubes and cells. Not in a world of gunfire and murder. The fact that her sister had been lying there with a bullet in her head all that time? She couldn't shake that mental image from her mind.

Even if the drunken father had been threatened, couldn't he have done something? Was everybody okay to let a body rot in the same house they lived in? Sure, it was more dried than rotted, but still, the insects and bugs had gone after it, and that would be a sight she would have a hard time getting rid of too. It seemed like it was emblazoned into her memory bank, probably for the rest of her life, along with the thought that her sister had come to such a terrible end.

Petra just shook her head, unable to get it all out of her brain. Finally, after washing her hair several times and scrubbing herself from top to bottom, she shut off the hot water, grabbed her towel, and dried off.

Cain was still out in the living room. Or was he? Had he left sometime in the night or early this morning? Or would she tiptoe out there to find him fast asleep, bent into a pretzel on that poor excuse of a couch? She hadn't had any extra money in the last year, since paying for her father's care and the research. Normal family members would have taken him in without the financial support, but, since her aunt wasn't willing to do that, and Petra couldn't afford the elderly home rates, this had been a good option. But no doubt it still took a huge dent out of her paycheck.

Deep down, she knew there was no real hope of getting her father back, and this was a lifestyle she had to maintain as long as he was in this state. His body was healthy, so it could go on for a long time.

That brought her mind back to Cain and his question about moving. Even if there were labs around the world where she could work on a cure, how could she possibly leave her father here? She didn't fool herself into thinking that he knew when she was there or that he was calmer or happier when she was around. She was just an assistant, giving him whatever sustenance his body needed. But, other than that, she had no relationship with her father anymore, no hint of her father, and that made her incredibly sad.

Dry, she tossed the towel up on a hook and walked into her bedroom fully nude, then pulled clothes out of her drawers. First panties and her white capri pants, then slipped into sandals, even as she strapped on her bra. After that she walked over for a simple turquoise T-shirt. Her hair was still wet, and she put it into a ponytail, high on the back of her head, knowing it made her look like she was eighteen years old. But she didn't really give a damn.

When she opened the bedroom door and walked out into the kitchen, she stopped, surprised to find Cain and Eton both sitting at the kitchen table. She looked at them, frowning.

Cain looked up and smiled when he saw her. He hopped up and walked over, wrapped her in his arms and held her close. Something about the look on his face told her something else had happened. She grabbed his forearms, her gaze going from Cain to Eton and back to Cain. "What happened?"

"Another blow in your life," he said. "Come over here

and sit down."

She resisted his pull toward the couch because, if it was bad news, she wanted to hear it now. But he insisted. Finally she dropped onto the couch and glared at him. "I'd rather hear bad news without being mollycoddled," she snapped.

He took a deep breath and said, "Okay. Listen, Petra. It's your father."

She took the blow viscerally, her body almost slamming into the back of the couch, as she stared at him in shock. "What about him?" she asked hesitantly, afraid to hear what he would say.

"He passed away in the night," he said.

She just stared at him and shook her head. "What? No. That can't be. His body was healthy. His mind was gone, but his body was healthy."

"That's something you'll have to take up with whoever does an autopsy, if one is even performed," he said.

She just stared at him, her mind trying to organize the words coming at her, but they weren't going together. "Wait. He's already been taken away?"

He took a deep breath again, settled down beside her, and said, "Look. I made a tough decision," he said. "Your father passed away in the wee hours of the night. I did hear about it, and I decided not to wake you." Then he stopped as if ready and willing to take whatever blow she was willing to hit him with.

She just continued to stare at him, in shock. "Why would you do that?"

"Because you'd been through enough already," he said gently. "You needed some quality sleep, and a chance to absorb some of the shock of one hit before another one hit you."

She sagged in place. "And he was already gone? They didn't call you to say that he was dying, that I could come say goodbye?" she asked helplessly.

"No," he said, "they did not. I don't have all the details. I just got a call saying your father had died."

She could only stare at him.

He nodded. "I know," he said. "As far as I am aware, he died of natural causes."

She snorted at that. "I'm not so sure about that," she said, turning to look out the window.

"Why not?" Eton asked intensely from the other side of the room.

She looked at him and hesitated.

He settled back slightly, as if aware of how intense his scrutiny was, and said, "If you have any doubts, suspicions, or accusations to make," he said, "this will be the only time you'll really have a chance to prove it one way or another."

"I was just always worried," she said.

"Worried about what?" Eton asked.

"He became this way after eating a meal with my aunt and uncle," she said. "And I have to admit, at the time, I was pretty suspicious that maybe Migi had poisoned him."

"Why would she do that?" Eton asked.

"It was after the accident, and he had a ways to go for a complete recovery, but he seemed to be okay. He had some money, and he had the house. My uncle had lost his job, and the bed-and-breakfast wasn't doing well, and my aunt and uncle were in danger of losing their house," she said. "It was just a wild thought. My uncle got sick at the same time but not as bad."

"Interesting, but it's hardly enough of a motive because they couldn't be guaranteed that they would get any of the money or the house, would they?"

"No," she said, "that's why I dismissed it."

"And why would it have brought on that kind of a condition?"

"He ended up without oxygen for a certain length of time," she said, "and, when they brought him back, he was like this."

"But haven't you been looking for a cure?"

"Yes," she said, "but he already had the markers for Alzheimer's. It just wasn't very developed. I was working on that, knowing that it probably wouldn't make any impact on his condition, because of the oxygen deprivation." She stared down at her hands. "I can't believe that my whole family is gone." Her voice held a helpless tone. "My sister and now my father."

"And even though it didn't happen at the same time, finding out at the same time is just as hard."

"It's essentially the same adjustment anyway."

"Yes, of course," he said. "And it doesn't make it any easier."

"No," she said, "if anything, it's much worse."

CAIN REMAINED BESIDE her, as Eton got up and put on a pot of coffee—their second but her first. Cain reached over and held her cold, clammy hands. "I'm sorry," he said, "I could have woken you in the night, but you couldn't do anything anyway."

"Maybe seen him before he went to the hospital," she said sadly. "But even then, maybe not. My aunt isn't exactly the friendliest of people." She frowned. "How did you find out? Did they call?" she asked, looking toward her phone on the counter.

"They would have, but Eton interrupted and said he would take care of it by calling me."

"I'm sure she'll have a bad attitude toward me today then."

"Why? Because I stayed at your apartment?"

She smiled and nodded. "Yes."

"Who cares what she thinks?" he said. "Particularly if you have doubts about her anyway."

"Right," she said. "I don't even know what to say. But I do want an autopsy done."

"You'll probably have to contact the coroner about that. I'm not sure what the budget is like here."

"It always comes down to money, doesn't it?" she said. "That was one of the other reasons why I had trouble with it being my aunt because she needed the money."

"You said that your uncle was sick too?"

"He just ended up with an upset stomach," she said, "but, in my uncle's case, it was different than my father's reaction. My father had some kind of attack that stopped the oxygen getting into his lungs. We thought he was dead, but the paramedics arrived really fast, and they brought him back," she said. "I was ecstatic, but he was never the same."

"Right, so it's possible it was premeditated. Did anybody ever check for poison?"

She shook her head. "By the time I thought to do it," she said, "months had passed."

"Which is too bad because you're working at a lab and might have had the facilities to test something like that."

"Oh, don't worry. I've chastised myself over that a lot. And now he's gone."

"The only good news in this scenario," Cain said, "and I

know it's not good news, is that you don't have to tell him about your sister."

"He wouldn't have understood anyway," she said. She sagged back into the couch, pulling her knees up tight against her chest and tucking her feet underneath. "I'm an orphan," she said in surprise.

"And, without your sister, then I gather, outside of your aunt, you have no other blood family?"

She shook her head. "No, just my aunt."

"So, they were brother and sister?"

"No," she said. "She was my mother's sister."

"What happened to your mother?"

"She died from childbirth complications after giving birth to my sister," she said quietly.

"So she hasn't been around for a very long time. And she's your only aunt? Right?"

"If you're asking about grandparents or other children, we have distant ties to Chico but other than that as far as I know, it's just the two of us."

"Interesting," he said. "I thought this region was known for big families."

"My family has never been particularly fertile or long-lived," she said. "My grandparents died when I was maybe nine or ten years old."

"How did they die?"

She looked at him and frowned. "There was an accidental fire, I believe."

"A lot of accidents," he said.

She looked at him, her tone hard. "I don't like my aunt much," she said, "but she is the only family I have. It's one thing for me to have suspicions, but—"

Eton chuckled. "But nobody else can, especially no observer coming at it from a completely detached point of view, right?"

"Of course you can," she said. "I just didn't really want to go down that pathway."

"Sometimes people do things we don't want to think about," he said.

"Who gained from your grandparents' death?" Cain asked.

"My aunt of course," she said. "My uncle has rarely worked in his life. Only in the last few years did he have more of a steady job. They live off their property. Then they sold off all the pieces to make it small enough that they could actually afford to be there. But then, at the same time, they sold off the gardens and orchards, so then they didn't have any income."

"Sounds like some of these deaths helped her out."

"Accidents and deaths, yes," she said.

"But your mother didn't die from anything suspicious at the hand of your aunt, right?"

"And to my knowledge neither did my grandparents," she said in a firm voice. "I shouldn't have brought up my suspicions about my father."

"Because none of it makes any sense?"

"No, it doesn't," she said, with a shrug.

"Except for the other factor. Is it possible any life insurance was on your father?"

"I don't think so," she said. "And, even so, it would come to me, not to her, right?"

A long silence followed, as Cain let her think about that. She got there and looked up at him. "Please tell me that you're not suggesting that she would kill me to get it."

"I'm not suggesting anything," he said quietly. "Unfortunately we've seen a whole lot more of the unpleasant side of life, so we don't want you to assume something that isn't there. Neither do we want you to be blind to something that could be there."

"Right," she groaned. "This isn't exactly the way I wanted to wake up this morning. But you know? I knew something was up. From the moment I woke up, something was telling me that the world as I'd known it had changed."

"On the other hand, you won't have to send a large chunk of your paycheck to your aunt now."

"Which is another reason why she wouldn't have done anything to hurt my father. She needed that income and still does."

"I get that, and she may not have had anything to do with this part, but, until we actually have a chance to go over there, we won't know."

She snorted at that. "If you think my aunt'll talk, you're wrong. She's always been extremely dominant in her attitude. She'll tell you what she wants you to know and nothing else."

"Well, after breakfast, I suggest we walk up and see her."

"She probably won't even let you into the house," she said. "After last night, I presume she asked you guys to leave?"

"And I came here with our gear this morning," Eton said. "So, essentially we've left already."

She nodded. "Are you leaving town today?"

"That's the plan," Cain said. "At least, it was, until your father died."

"That doesn't change anything for you," she said, reaching up and rubbing her forehead. "I, on the other hand, now have two deaths to deal with. Funerals, law enforcement, and coroner. One of the things that disturbs me the most. Not only did she come back to town and didn't see her family but she's been in that bedroom for how long?" She shook her head. "And to think that old man Morgan knew about it." She shook her head. "It just defies logic."

"When people are afraid, they do all kinds of things," he said. "There's often absolutely nothing you can do or say to calm somebody down. They'll do whatever they choose because, to them, it is literally a fight of survival. But, before the day starts," he said, as Eton poured a cup of coffee and brought it to her, "we'll have a little bit of downtime to have some coffee and some real food."

She nodded slowly. "I need to write down a list of everything to do," she said. "I've got a ton of details to take care of."

He reached out and squeezed her fingers. "If you need us to stay an extra day—"

She looked at him, with a small smile. "As much as I would love to have that kind of emotional support, you guys are on a mission yourselves. You don't have the time. I'm not sure what this is all about here and how it affects you, but it's obvious that you made a trip here for some interrelated reason."

"We did," he said, "and now we'll track down this Tristan. Any ideas, besides his father's place?"

"You know what? Those kids had different mothers, and Tristan's mom remarried and lives here in town."

He stopped and looked at her. "What's her new name?"

"Monteith, is his name. They've been married about five years or so, I think." She settled back with her cup of coffee, but a frown was on her face.

Cain waited for a long moment. "What is it? What are

you thinking?"

She tilted her head to the side and looked at him. "I don't know much about her, but her husband's another one of those very unsettling men," she said. "Looks more like a thug than anything."

"Do you think he's one of Tristan's gang?"

"No. I'd want to say Tristan's one of his because I can't stand the man," she said quietly. "But that's not fair. I don't believe he's connected to this mess, no."

"Sounds like something I need to get into then," Eton said. "Everything's kind of on hold, until we sort out this new wrinkle."

"Did you actually have a location to disappear to?" she asked the guys.

"Not yet," Cain said. "That was next."

"Well," she said, "today will be a shit day anyway. You might as well get all your ducks in a row, before you fly off in the wrong direction."

He looked at her, smiled, and said, "What about you? Where will you start?"

"With my aunt. After I get a decent meal, I'll go to her and see exactly what the hell happened."

CHAPTER 9

A<small>ND THAT'S EXACTLY</small> what Petra did. After a small breakfast of fresh fruit and yogurt, the men insisted on eggs and toast. Then she walked to her aunt's house, with Cain at her side. She looked at him. "You don't have to come with me, you know?"

"I want to," he said. "I want to see what exactly is going on here and see if I can figure it out."

"Until we get an autopsy report," she said, "chances are we won't hear very much."

"Maybe not," he said, "but we'll go take a look, shall we?"

She smiled and nodded. "Thanks," she said.

"Thanks for what?"

"Letting me sleep," she said. "Assuming there was nothing I could have done to help him, and I couldn't say goodbye because he was already gone, then you were right. I needed some rest pretty badly after last night."

"Will you tell your aunt about your sister?"

Her steps faltered at that. She shoved her hands into the pockets of her light sweater and said, "I'm not sure. But you know how news travels, so she'll find out somehow. I guess she should hear it from me."

The B&B was up ahead.

"You know something? It looks so innocent and inconspicuous," she said. "It used to be a large property here, all by itself, but, with them slowly selling off parts, and other properties being built up around it, it became this."

"A lot of farmers did that," Cain said. "You can work the land—as long as it brings a profit and as long as you're young and healthy, where you can afford to expend the physical work. But, once that starts to fail, it doesn't leave you with a whole lot left."

"I'm not sure Migi ever worked," she said. "She planned to have a family, but they never did have any children."

"That's too bad," he said. "But, if she worked the land with him, there's only so much money you can eke out for a living. Eventually something else looks a whole lot easier."

"And that would be her too," Petra said. "I've struggled with just so many things about her. But she's the only family I've got."

"I'm sorry about that," he said.

She smiled with a nod. "We'll be sorry, until it's all over with," she said. "But it doesn't change anything, does it?" She groaned. "So, I've got to tell you that this conversation with Migi? I don't know how it'll go."

"Don't worry about it," he said. "I've seen and heard a lot in my life. Nothing'll surprise me at this point."

"I get it," she said, "but my aunt may not be the warmest."

"She should be," he said. "She's the only family you've got. She's looked after your father for a number of months. She needed your money."

"I understand, but I don't know what we'll be facing when we get there." As it was, her uncle sat outside on her father's chair, slowly rocking. She made her way up the steps and sat down on a rocker beside him. "Are you okay?"

He looked at her, and his eyes were older than she'd ever seen them before and were sad, so very sad. He nodded slowly. "He just wasn't there from one moment to the next," he said. "I was calling to him to get him up to bed, and, when I touched him, he was already gone."

She smiled with a nod. "You know that there are worse ways to go."

"There are, indeed," he said. "I was just so hoping that it wasn't true."

"What?"

"That he was gone, of course," he said.

"How's your wife?" Cain asked.

The old man looked at him. "She's the way she always is. She's in there, baking up a storm."

"Did the doctor say anything when they picked him up?" Petra asked.

"It was the paramedics," he said. "And, no, they just collected the body and disappeared." He looked at her. "You have to decide what you want to do with him now."

"No decision needed," she said. "He'll be buried in the family graveyard, beside my mother."

Her uncle smiled, patted her hand, and said, "You've been a good daughter."

"I tried," she said. "But, ever since that accident, it's been pretty hard."

"I know. It's been hard for us all." That was almost the first time he'd ever made mention of how hard it was to look after her father, and she realized just how much he, too had been emotionally bonded to her father. The two men had been together for a long time. "You did a good job helping him," she said, kissing him on the cheek. "Thank you."

He smiled, but a wateriness came to his eyes. "It feels

like everything's different now," he said.

"I was thinking the same thing," she said. "Everything's changed."

"It has."

She got up and walked in to see her aunt in the kitchen. She called out, "Good morning."

Her aunt spun in shock and immediately glared at her. "Oh, you finally decided to show up, did you? Shows how much you care."

"And is my father here now? No, of course not," Petra said. "So what was the point of coming early?"

"No, that's quite true," her aunt said. "But you didn't come last night either, did you?"

"I didn't wake her," Cain said easily.

"Sleeping together?" she said, with a sniff. "What is it with young people today?"

"I don't know," Cain said. "What *is* with young people today?"

She glared at him and said, "Good thing you're gone."

"And thank you for your kind hospitality," he said, with a genial smile, as if missing the barb of her words.

Migi just sniffed again, banging pans around.

"I came to clean up my father's room," Petra said.

Her aunt stiffened, spun, and glared at her. "Is that all you think about?"

Petra stared at her aunt in shock. "What are you talking about?" she asked. "You haven't wanted him here since the beginning, so I came to get rid of his stuff for you, while I had somebody to help carry things."

"Whatever," she said. "Go. Go get it all. Nothing's there worth keeping anyway."

"And how would you know?" Petra asked.

Her aunt just sniffed.

With a motion toward Cain, she turned and led the way back around the kitchen and up the stairs. As they got to the top of the stairs, he thought he heard some footsteps down below. He leaned over the railing and saw the aunt standing at the base of the stairs, glaring up at them. He turned to Petra and held his fingers to his lips and motioned at Petra.

Petra walked over, took one look, and rolled her eyes. She went into her father's room, closed the door, and whispered, "Like I said, no love lost here."

"It's sad," he said. He looked around the room. "Is there anything to pack his clothes into?"

"Well, a suitcase was here, but I'm not sure if it's here now." She opened up the closet, dug into what was on the floor, and pulled out a bag. "This'll do," she said. "I'll take his clothes to the church when I go into town."

With Cain's help, she quickly packed up all her father's clothing. She found no personal belongings to be seen anywhere. Nothing. She frowned at that. "I had pictures of my mother in here and some of his personal mementos. I wonder what happened to those."

He just stood by, not saying anything.

She glanced at him. "Do you think Migi got rid of them?"

"Your aunt isn't exactly the warmest and most loving person on the block," he said, "so I've no idea."

She turned and checked the closet again. "Nothing's here. It's completely empty now," she said. "Can you check on top of the shelf? And I'll check under the bed."

They went through the motions, but there didn't appear to be anything else to be found. Finally she shrugged and said, "Well, that's very depressing. I brought those things to make him feel like he wasn't so alone."

"Was he aware?"

"No, he wasn't, but that doesn't necessarily mean that he wouldn't have found some comfort. That was the whole reason for it."

"Well, let's go ask your aunt then," he said.

She looked around and said, "We're not missing anything, right?"

"Nothing here to miss," he said. "It's really bare in here."

"Totally bare." She took a deep breath, motioned at the bag, and said, "Would you mind?"

He grabbed it and said, "Let's go."

As they went down the stairs, her aunt scurried away from the base of the bottom of the stairs, back into the kitchen. Petra rolled her eyes at that. As she walked into the kitchen, she said, "Where are his personal belongings?"

"What do you mean?" she said.

"I mean, the pictures of Mom and the other stuff that I brought from the house to be with him."

"He got mad one day and threw it out," she said dismissively.

She looked at her aunt in surprise. "You never told me about that."

"So what?" she said. "Besides, he didn't need a picture of her sitting there. She's been gone twenty years."

"Longer than that actually, but he never remarried because he never fell in love with anybody else," she said in a smooth voice. "So you had absolutely no reason not to leave it sitting there."

"Well, I didn't do anything with it," she said, "so don't go accusing me of anything."

"I'm not accusing you," Petra said. "I'm just asking."

"Says you," she said, with a big sniff. "Go take your little boyfriend and leave."

"Oh, absolutely," she said. "Have a nice life."

As he walked out to the front door, Cain asked, "Do you want to go back and say something about your sister?"

She glared at him but understood the sense of it. She shrugged. "Maybe I'll tell my uncle instead."

As she walked outside, she saw her uncle, still sitting there, a forlorn look on his face. She sat down in front of him. "Unfortunately I have more bad news to share."

He looked up at her and said, "More?"

She sighed. "Yes, I'm sorry." Then she told him about her sister.

He just stared at her in shock. "Both of them?"

"Yes," she said. "Both of them."

This time there were tears in his eyes. He reached up and wiped them away. "You know? I thought I saw her a few months back, but I couldn't believe it. When I called out, she didn't answer me, so I figured I was wrong."

"Really?"

"Yes," he said. "I'm sorry. It must have been somebody else."

"Well," she said, "hopefully we'll find answers as to why she was here."

"I hope so," he said, "because that is very sad. She had so much to live for."

"I know, but she was also not very happy with us," she said sadly. "And now it's too late to do anything about it, and I've lost both of them."

He shook his head. "It's a sad, sad world."

"Who was she with?" Cain asked.

He shrugged. "She was in a vehicle. I didn't see who was

driving and didn't recognize the truck."

"What do you know about a guy named Monteith?" she asked. "He married Tristan's mom?"

"Bad news," he said. "The way I see it, that whole family is bad news."

"Were they involved in Tristan's business?"

"I don't think so, but they're living high on the hog," he said, "in an area where none of the rest of us are doing very well at all." He looked at Petra. "I have no idea what we're supposed to do now."

"I'm sorry," she said. "I know looking after my father helped you pay the bills."

He nodded slowly. "That it did. But your father was my friend, and I would have done it for nothing."

"Well, *you* might have," she said with a small smile.

He acknowledged the notion with a nod, then shook his head back and forth. "She is who she is, but deep down there is a good woman inside."

Petra nodded wistfully and turned to walk away.

Cain looked back at him and said, "Does anybody here have life insurance?"

Her uncle looked at Cain in surprise. "I got some way back when," he said. "But I don't think your father did, did he?"

She looked at him and frowned. "I haven't been paying for any," she said, "so I don't think so."

"It's something we'll have to look into," Cain noted.

She turned, looked back at her uncle, and said, "I'm surprised that you had some."

"I set it up a long time ago," he said. "It wasn't very much back then, but it sure has been hard to pay for these last many years."

"Are you still paying for it?" she asked.

He nodded. "I can't take the chance of leaving her with nothing," he said.

She smiled, nodded. "You are a good man."

"Well, sometimes I am," he said, "but it hasn't felt like it lately."

"You're okay," she said.

He just shrugged and started moving the rocker back and forth. She turned and headed down the road again. As they walked away, she said, "Why did you ask him about life insurance?"

Cain smiled and said, "Honestly I'm wondering if whatever happened to your father was meant to happen to her husband, so the life insurance could be claimed."

She shuddered. "You guys must inhabit a world full of very unpleasant things."

"Indeed," he said. "But it is what it is."

"Do you think it could actually be something like that?"

"No way to know yet," he said. "We'll have to take another look into it."

"I don't want to deal with that," she said. "That doesn't sound like something I want to get involved in."

"Maybe," he said. "But you want to know the truth, right?"

"I'm not sure," she said. "That sounds like a waste of time and energy because what can we do about it now?"

"True," he said, and he stayed quiet.

They kept walking.

Then she added, "It'll drive me nuts now. You know that."

"Yep," he said, "I figured it would."

She groaned. "I almost prefer not knowing anything."

DALE MAYER

"Yeah," he said. "I get it. But you have to make a decision about it before too many things happen."

"True," she whispered. "I need to call the coroner, I
guess."

"You do. And the cops."

"Cops? I don't think there'll be any kind of investiga-
tion," she said, "so I don't suspect there's any problem with
that."

"A phone call won't hurt."

"If you say so," she said.

As soon as they walked into her house, Eton looked up
expectantly. She shrugged and said, "There wasn't anything
to learn, except that apparently my uncle has life insurance."
At that, Eton's face lit up. She frowned at him. "Why does
that make you happy?"

"Because I highly suspect that the original attempt was
to take out your uncle," he said. "And now that you've
confirmed the existence of life insurance, I should be able to
find it."

She shook her head. "Is that all you do? Pry into other
people's lives?"

"Lots of times. Yes," he said, "that's exactly what I do.
But only because we have to."

She nodded. "I just don't like that type of a world."

"None of us do," he said.

Petra walked over and put on the teakettle and stared
outside. Pulling out her phone, she looked up the number
she wanted and dialed it. As soon as she got through to the
coroner's office, she asked about her father.

"His body can be released this afternoon," the man said.
"Let us know what funeral home you want him to go to."

"I will, thanks," she said. "Is there a cause of death?"

110

"His heart stopped," the guy said on the other side. "Nothing else."

She hung up, looked at Cain, and told him what he said.

"Kind of to be expected, right?"

"Maybe," she said. "I didn't ask about an autopsy."

"You can if you want to," he said.

"I know. I'm just not sure I want to get into it."

"That's up to you to decide," they both said in sync.

She smiled, nodded, and finally just couldn't let it go. She pulled her phone back out and called again. "Are you doing an autopsy on my father?"

"No," the man came back. "Cause of death has already been cleared. No need to."

"He had a mental problem," she said, "but physically he was strong."

"No. Anybody with the lack of oxygen episode he had with his original brain injury isn't as strong as they may appear," the man said in a sympathetic tone. "They often have problems and a much shorter life span."

"What would it take to get an autopsy done?"

"Is there a reason to suspect anything?" His voice came back sharper.

"No, I don't have any specific reason, except that he just suddenly died."

"And that happens," he said. "I'm very sorry, and I understand that it's difficult, but that doesn't make it wrong. If you want an autopsy at this point, you'd have to get it done through a private firm."

"Well, I'll have to give that some thought." She hung up and walked back into the kitchen, telling the men about it.

"That's kind of what we expected," he said. "Very few cases are actually given full autopsies these days."

"Do we suspect foul play?" she asked, sitting down at the kitchen table with a hard *thump*. "I mean, is there any serious reason to suspect that my aunt or my uncle might have had something to do with my father's death?"

The two men looked at her. Cain then spoke. "We don't have any proof obviously, so I'm not sure anything would trigger something like an autopsy."

"Even if you just got a tox screen done though," Eton said, "that would let you know if any drugs were in his system."

"There shouldn't have been any drugs," she said. "He took no prescriptions." She pulled her phone out yet again and called, asking to speak to the coroner again. When he came on the line, she said, "It's me again. I'm very sorry to bother you. Is there any way we can at least do a tox screen?"

"Why is this an issue?"

"Because I need to know," she said, "for myself." She heard a heavy sigh on the other end.

"I'll see what I can do," he said, "but remember, it takes months to get the results."

Petra winced at that. "Okay," she said, "and thank you." She hung up and told the other two.

"That makes sense, but at least then you'll know," Cain said.

"Right. And, if they do that, then I can go ahead with the funeral arrangements."

"Do you have any idea what your father wanted?"

"Yes," she said. "There's no will. All his personal effects, house, and everything were sold already to help pay for his care."

"But you retain control of that?" Cain asked her.

She nodded. "He put my name on his accounts a long

time ago, so, if anything ever happened to him, I'd have access to it without going through a big legal process. Why?"

"Just wanted to make sure. What kind of money are we talking about?"

Because he asked in a clear, concise way, she answered the same way. "He actually inherited from his family as well, so quite a bit of money is in there, over a half million US dollars. I haven't been using it because I thought he would live a long time and would someday require a skilled nursing scenario. So I've been covering his expenses myself."

"So those assets are now yours then?" Eton asked.

"Yeah, I guess so."

Cain then asked, "And, if something happens to you, then what?"

She looked at them. "Then it goes to my aunt." She stopped, sat back in her chair, and whispered, "Oh, shit."

Both men nodded, looking very serious.

"IT'S SOMETHING YOU need to be aware of," Cain said. "There's just you left, and, if your aunt or uncle know how much money there is, and they know that your sister's gone now, that means that they are the only ones left, besides you. Which means, in theory, your life could be in danger."

"It's unbelievable," she said. "I would never have suspected or looked at my family in this way at all. My aunt has always been harsh and bitter, but I never would have thought she would hurt me."

"I know, and I'm sorry," Cain said, "but it's something that you do need to keep an eye on."

"Wow! That doesn't make staying here look like a very positive proposition."

"I wouldn't advise it," he said, "but you'd need another place to go to that would make you feel like it could be home."

"I don't have any place that's home," she said. "This is home."

"Understood. But sometimes, sometimes it's easier to stay because you don't have any other plans. But, in that case, it'll play right into your aunt's hands. I mean, it may not be right away. It could be another year from now. What if you're doing something, and all of a sudden you have an accident? What if you suddenly get food poisoning?" he asked. "There are so many ways to take out a person. All she has to do is bide her time."

"I really don't like your view of my aunt," she whispered.

The trouble was, he'd seen it too many times. "All I'm saying is, be careful." Just then, both guys' phones rang. Cain looked at Eton, as they pulled out their phones. "Ice, what's up?"

"Your Tristan landed in Rome, rented a vehicle, and is headed your way."

"Good. Let him come," he said. "Any idea if he knows we're here with Petra?"

"Hard to say, but, since we tracked his movements, I'm sure he or somebody above him is tracking yours."

"Great."

"Any news on your end?"

"Well, it's gotten a little complicated." He moved a few steps away, so he wouldn't upset Petra with his monologue and quickly gave Ice a synopsis of what was going on in the small town.

"The sister's been in the bedroom for how long?"

"We're not exactly sure," he said. "Definitely a few

months, it seems. But, with Petra's father passing last night, things got even more complicated."

"Are they connected?"

"You know what? If it weren't for everything else going on, I'd say no," he said.

"How does that even possibly work?"

"Right," he said. "It makes absolutely no sense at the moment, but we're hoping that we'll get to the bottom of it."

"True," she said. "Let me know if you need any help with it because we can't have this kind of crap going on everywhere."

"Nope, we can't," he said. "Hopefully we'll come up with some answers very quickly." When he hung up with Ice, he turned and walked back to the others.

"I'm glad you have a team around you," Petra said.

"We'll need it apparently," Cain said. "Tristan landed in Rome late last night and is heading here."

"And how would your people know that? That's a hell of a long way away."

"He flew into Rome, probably to establish an alibi for killing the cop, then rented a vehicle, and they're tracking it."

"Not exceeding the speed limit, it'll take him about seven hours to get here. So why drive?" she asked, looking puzzled.

"To hide his tracks," he said smoothly.

"And yet it didn't," she pointed out.

Cain chuckled. "No, but we have a pretty wide net that we're casting," he said. "So he has to think as wide as we are."

"Jesus," Petra said. "I can't wrap my head around all

this."

"It's all good," he said.

"How could it be good?" she asked, shaking her head. "Is he coming after someone?"

"Maybe," he said. "What about you and making your calls?"

"I've contacted the funeral home to make arrangements for my father. I probably could have a memorial at the same time for my sister, but I haven't gotten that far yet," she said. "Regardless, it'll just be a small family gathering. Most of the people who my dad knew from here aren't around anymore anyway. The small town I grew up in was very different from what it is now."

"Of course," he said.

She said, "So, in my case, everything is moving forward."

"And your sister's autopsy?"

"Yes. I need to call about that too. But, in that case, I probably need to talk to the police first because I don't know when—well, you know."

Just then, her phone rang. She groaned and whispered, "It's the police." He listened, while she talked to somebody quietly, then said, "Yes. I'll come straight down." She hung up her phone, looked at the other two, and said, "Well, you get to stay here, while I get to be questioned about my sister now."

"Don't let them bully you," Cain said. "You're the one who's fully justified to be asking them for answers. The fact that they won't have very many doesn't change that fact."

She smiled, nodded, and stood. "God, what a shitty day."

"Want company?"

She looked at him in surprise.

He frowned, tilted his head, and said, "You don't have to be strong all the time, you know?"

"Will you stop them from badgering me?"

He chuckled. "Me just being there is likely to do that," he said.

She hesitated, shook her head, and said, "I'll be fine." She walked to the front door. There she stopped.

"You might be fine, but that doesn't mean you have to do it alone."

She turned, looked back at him, caught Eton's expression, then looked back at Cain, and said, "If you wouldn't mind, I could use the company."

"I wouldn't mind in the least." He hopped to his feet and handed his laptop to Eton. "I've got my phone. Keep in touch."

Eton smiled, nodded, and said, "See if you can find out anything useful while you're at it, huh?"

Cain walked up behind her, opened the door, then closed it behind them, after they stepped through.

"You sure you don't mind?" she asked, chewing on her lip.

"Not only do I not mind," he said, "I relish the opportunity. I've dealt with the police a lot in my life."

"That surprises me," she said with a laugh. "I'd have figured you to be the kind of guy always avoiding the police."

"Oh, I do that too," he said. "But mostly because their job and my job don't always align very well."

"Shouldn't it though? Aren't you on the same team?"

"Yes, that's true, and maybe it should," he said, "but the devil is in the details. They don't always approve of our methods."

"True," she said. "Still, it's not helpful."

"Nope. Let's go," he said. "Do we walk or drive?"

She frowned. "Let's drive," she said.

He nodded and took her hand. "Let's make it look as if we're friends."

"Actually I was counting you as one," she said. She squeezed his fingers and pointed to her car up front. "Let's go."

CHAPTER 10

WHEN PETRA PARKED behind the police station, she took a deep breath and said, "I don't know why this is bothering me so much."

"It should bother you," he said. "Just think about it. You've been to hell and back, and somebody has done this to your sister and left her there. Then, at the same time, you've also endured the loss of your father. What could the police and their questions possibly do to you at this point? They surely can't do any more to you than life has done already."

She chuckled at that. "Are you sure?"

"Well, no," he said, "because it can surely be a pain in the ass to deal with some of these people."

"True," she said, "but let's go." She led the way inside, and, as she walked in, she went to the woman behind the desk and introduced herself, saying she was here to see Detective Conus.

The woman smiled and said, "Take a seat. I'll let him know you're here."

At that, Petra walked over and took a seat on a hard bench. After a few minutes, the bench started to bite into her butt. "Seems like they could spring for more comfortable seating, if they'll make us wait out here," she muttered.

"I think it's part of the plan," he said, chuckling.

She smiled. "Maybe so, but it's still a pain in the ass.

Literally."

"Yep, it is."

A moment later the door opened, and a detective stood there, looking at her, waving her in. The two of them walked toward him. He looked up at Cain and asked, "And who are you?"

His accent was thick and broken. Cain answered in kind, introducing himself. "I'm a friend of Petra's," he said.

The detective looked at Petra, and she looked back with a steady stare. He just shrugged and said, "Well, come in then, if she wants you here." As they walked inside a nearby office, and everybody was seated, the detective asked, "When did you last hear from your sister?"

"I told you last night, not for many months. Apparently though my uncle thinks he saw her not too long ago."

"Seriously?" The detective raised his head from making notes and looked at both of them.

"According to what the uncle said this morning, yes," Cain said.

"Okay, I'll have to talk to him about that then," he said.

"Perfect," she said. "As for me and my sister, I haven't seen her since right before she left, about eighteen months ago. Last time we talked face-to-face, she left, upset and angry."

"Why?"

"She was pregnant," Petra said bluntly. "So I don't know if she aborted the baby or had it and gave it up for adoption or what."

"Interesting," he said. "Who else can confirm this?"

"My uncle, most likely," she said.

"About the pregnancy?"

She shrugged. "I don't know how much my uncle knew

or didn't know about that," she said.

"And your aunt?" Detective Conus asked.

"Same thing."

"Your father?"

At that, she felt something inside her crumble.

Cain immediately reached across, grabbed her hand, and told the detective, "Her father passed away last night."

The detective's gaze widened. "I'm sorry. I didn't know that. Can you tell me what happened?"

She nodded, composed herself, and said, "Apparently, just from one moment to the next, he was gone. I found out this morning. His body is at the morgue right now."

The detective made several notations on his notepad. "I'll check into it," he said.

She nodded.

He continued, "Can you tell me anything about your sister?"

"She hooked up with Chico," she said. "And, after that, everything went to hell and back."

"I'm sorry, and she was found in Chico's house, correct?"

She looked at him. "Technically speaking, it was Chico's father's house, but Chico did live there, at least part of the time. And my sister was found in Chico's bedroom. But, unless you're new here, we both already knew that, as did everybody else in town."

"Just trying to get as much information as I can," he said quietly.

She nodded, not saying anything, but, from her perspective, he was being deliberately obtuse.

He looked at Cain. "How long have you been here?'

"Not very long," he said. "Why?"

"Just wondered what you might have had to do with any of this."

"Nothing," he said. "I was staying at her aunt and uncle's bed-and-breakfast."

"And what made you choose that bed-and-breakfast?"

"I came here on business," he said, "and I was looking to enjoy the flavor of the town," he spoke easily, the words rolling off his tongue smoothly.

But something about it the detective didn't like. "I might need references from you."

"And why is that?"

The detective didn't have an answer.

"You're welcome to have them," Cain said. He brought out his phone and handed off Ice's name and number.

"Relationship?"

"Business associate and friend," he said.

"I suspect you're in town for a whole different reason."

"Well, I don't know about that," he said. "I would think that Chico would be at the top of your list too."

"Chico has a bad rep in town," the detective said, "but he's never been charged with anything." There was almost a word of warning in his voice.

Cain gave him a saber-toothed smile and said, "That's nice. And why is that?"

The detective stiffened at that. "We don't like troublemakers here," he snapped.

"Good," he said, "because I'm not one. But it seems like a few people around here are."

"You don't know what you're talking about," he said.

"Maybe, maybe not, but we'll see what happens when we look at the autopsy report on that young woman found in Chico's bedroom. His father was there in the house the whole time."

"You think we'll look at him for this too?"

"I doubt that he was anything other than drunk for most of the time," she snapped.

"It doesn't matter what you think," the detective said. "We'll need evidence."

"That would be good," Cain said softly, but no doubt something very deadly was behind it. "A lot of the world will be watching this case."

At that, the detective looked at him, clearly startled. "Why is that?" he asked. "What's this got to do with anybody beyond this town?"

"It has a lot to do with a lot of people," he said. "You might want to keep that in mind, when you start dealing with it."

"We don't take kindly to threats," he said stiffly.

"No threat intended," he said. "Just saying you might want to keep it in mind."

The detective asked a few more questions, but it was obvious he'd lost his will to proceed.

As she stood, Petra said, "I want a copy of the autopsy report."

"Well, you can't have it," he said. "When the autopsy is completed, you can have the death certificate with a cause of death. But the autopsy report is not available to the public."

"And why is that?" Cain asked.

"Because we don't want details going out before we've charged somebody for this crime."

"And didn't you just say you were looking at Chico's father for that?"

The detective looked at him and said, "The case is open until solved."

"Be interesting to see what you end up with," Cain said.

"The truth," he snapped. "I'm not sure what you think we're doing here, but it won't be anything other than what can be justified by evidence."

"It sounds like maybe the evidence will not prove anything," she snapped. "My sister was shot, and obviously Chico shot her. But I can see needing to have some evidence to support that theory."

"Obviously," he said. "And, like I said, the father's still there too."

"Sure enough," she said. "I'll leave it in your hands. And I do want my sister's body released as soon as possible."

"Oh, it will be," he said. He looked at Cain. "And how long are you staying in town?"

"Just a day or two," he said. "Long enough to see this through." And he shot the detective a hard look. The detective immediately opened his mouth, and Cain shook his head. "Don't even go there," he said. "I can reach the next ten people above you in this district alone," he said. "This *will* be handled properly." And, with that, he motioned Petra toward the door. "Come on. No further point in being here."

"If you say so," she said. As they walked outside, she asked, "Can you really reach up that high?"

"Absolutely," he said. "But that doesn't mean I want to."

"Of course not."

SOMETHING WAS ODD about the whole thing. Cain sent Ice a brief text message. **Not sure what's going on, a cover-up in the making maybe.** He didn't get an answer right away, and he didn't expect one.

"Will it make any difference?" Petra asked.

"No idea. But let's make sure your sister gets justice. That's what I would like to see."

"She was young and flighty, but that doesn't mean she doesn't deserve justice," Petra said. "I wish we could figure out what happened to the baby," she whispered. "That's the thing that really haunts me now."

"How old would it be by now?"

She thought about it, shrugged, and said, "You know what? It's so hard, since I don't know exactly how far along she was. But, based on my father's accident and her leaving both being eighteen months ago, I would guess the baby is less than a year for sure, probably not even that."

"Anybody interested in the family who could have a newborn child like that?"

"I don't think so," she said.

"What about medical facilities, where she could have had an abortion?"

"Well, they certainly exist. I just don't know which one or where."

"We could always take a quick look and see what we can come up with," Cain said.

"Hardly part of your workload," she said.

He pulled out his phone and sent Ice a text. "It's okay. It's a part of the larger picture. We'll need access to her social security number or whatever the equivalent is over here."

"Okay," she said, "I have all that at home."

He said, "Good. We can probably sort it out fast enough."

Once they got back, Eton looked up at them. She sighed. "It's lunchtime. I need something for my stomach acids to work on."

"That bad?"

"Well, definitely not good," she said. "Not to mention the fact that the detective seemed very suspicious of Cain being here."

"We're used to that," Eton said. "It goes with the business."

She walked into the bedroom, pulled out her box of paperwork, and came back with one of her sister's tax returns. "I have been hanging on to these for a while," she said. "I used to help her, way back when, before she hated me."

"What are we looking for?" Eton asked when she handed a document to him.

"Whether she had an abortion."

"Right," he said. "That should be fast."

She shook her head. "It shouldn't be fast. Some things should be private."

"Do you want some privacy?"

"No, but that doesn't mean it shouldn't be private, at least harder to get to that info," she said.

"Is it covered by medical here?"

"Oh, I hadn't thought of that," she said. "Yes, it would have been."

It didn't take him but about twenty minutes. "She had an abortion almost eighteen months ago."

Petra sat down heavily. "Well, in a sense, that's good news, I guess, since I won't always have to keep looking over my shoulder to see if I missed a family member somewhere. I hate the thought of a child abandoned because of my sister's murder," she said.

"Well, the autopsy should also prove the fact that she didn't have a child," he said. "So let's make sure we check on that."

She nodded. "Good point. They should be able to see something like that."

"Absolutely."

With that, she pulled out ingredients for sandwiches. She fixed five huge sandwiches, dishing up two for Cain and two for Eton. She dug into hers, not waiting for the guys. Everybody was quiet, probably realizing Petra needed the fuel. Finally she said to Eton, "Did you find out anything while we were gone?"

"Yep. Tristan's almost to town now," he said.

She looked at him in shock. "Seriously?"

He nodded. "I'm pretty sure the trigger on the door we went through, when we found your sister's body, didn't just trigger the neighbor cop. It also brought Tristan running, who then killed the cop. Tristan's coming now to make an appearance, like he wasn't here before."

Petra stared at Cain, knowing he was holding something back. "So he's coming to clean up then?"

"That would be my guess, yes."

"Gross," she said. "I'm not sure I'm up to dealing with him."

"Do you know him?"

"Yes, but only in passing because he's Patina's brother. He's older than Patina and Chico and hasn't been around here much that I know of."

"Well, you'll probably have a chance to form a new impression," he said with a smile. "Because I guarantee you, he'll be here very soon." He checked on the security cameras going through town. "Like in less than five minutes."

She stared at him in shock. "He's coming *here*? To my apartment?"

"Well, he's in the parking lot right now." They both

crowded around the laptop and watched as he came out of the vehicle and headed toward her front door. Sure enough, two minutes later came a knock on the door.

Cain hopped up and reached the door before her. She glared at him. He shook his head and said, "He's armed." He opened the door wide, startling the man on the other side. When the newcomer glared at him, Cain crossed his arms over his chest and said, "What can I do for you?" He spoke in a long slow drawl he'd perfected a long time ago.

The man frowned in confusion. He gazed around Cain, behind him, until Tristan's gaze landed on Petra. Then he smiled. "Petra!" he said, trying to step forward.

But Cain didn't budge, leaving the newcomer no place to move.

She walked forward. "Tristan?"

"Yes," he said. "How are you?"

"I'm fine," she said, "or I will be when I recover from the recent losses in my family, which I've only just found out about."

He frowned, as if not understanding.

She snapped, "My sister, dead with a bullet hole in her head, in Chico's bedroom at your father's house."

He just stared at her in shock.

Cain had to give him kudos for his ability to act. But then Tristan had probably had a long time to practice this.

"Will you deny that you didn't know my sister was dead and stored in a bedroom in your father's house? Was it Chico who killed her, or was it you?"

"I didn't kill your sister," he said immediately. "And why would I leave her in Chico's bedroom? That's just—" He shook his head. "I can't imagine what that looks like now."

"It's disgusting," she said. "An abomination, so very

wrong on many levels."

"I'm sorry. My father is not in good mental health," he said, immediately pointing the finger at the old drunk. "As you well know, he's spent much of the last few years drunk."

"Well, he's certainly spent much of the last few months drunk," she said, "which is about how long my sister has been lying there."

"Of course," he said. "That would be very logical. After he killed her, he was overcome with grief."

"That's funny it happened around the same time Chico left," she said. "When were you here last, Tristan? You liked her too, didn't you?"

"You know how I travel a lot for my business."

Cain studied the man. Something was just a little too slick, a little too smarmy about him. Swarthy complexion, dark hair. It was as if the rich life had gotten into his system, and now he looked seedy and swollen.

Cain looked down at Petra and then back at Tristan.

"What about the guy who shot at us?" she said.

He put his hand to his chest and stepped backward. "What do you mean? Somebody shot at you?"

"Well, an alarm was set to go off if a certain door in your father's house was opened, which was triggered to the house next door," Cain said smoothly, not giving an inch. "Within minutes we had the shooter. Somebody associated with you."

"I have a lot of connections in town," he said. "Also I'm no longer associated with a lot of people. Our bad childhood resulted in connections I don't care to continue."

"Well, that might work for you," Cain said in a crisp tone. "It won't work for me though."

"And you are?"

Cain smiled and said, "The name's Cain. But then you

already know that. Since you hired Chico and others to take me and my friends out in Perth."

There was a movement in the back of his eye, ever-so-slight, but enough for Cain to have caught it because he was looking very closely. Cain smiled, finding Tristan's tell.

Immediately Tristan shook his head. "You have me mistaken for somebody else," he said. "Absolutely no way I hired anybody to try to kill you."

He gave such a great imitation of being shocked that Cain knew most people would have serious doubts. But not him. He'd seen guys like this, many of them over the last ten years. He just gave him a hard smile. "Well, as you can see, I'm not so easy to kill," he said.

Tristan gave him a look of active dislike, then turned to Petra. "Can we talk?"

She hesitated and then motioned to the apartment. "Come on in."

But Tristan didn't budge. He said, "Can we talk without him?"

"Why?" she asked, looking puzzled. And Cain had to give it to her. She was doing a very good job of playing the innocent.

"Because I don't like him," he said.

"Well, I don't have any problem with him being around," she said. "As a matter of fact, after being shot at, I feel much safer."

"You don't honestly think I had something to do with that, do you?"

"After finding my sister dead in Chico's bedroom," she said, "I'm not exactly sure what to think."

"It wasn't me," he said. "Think about it. How will that even work? Everything was locked from the inside—as I understand."

"And how would you know that?" Cain asked.

"The cops," he said instantly. "I figure your sister proba-bly committed suicide."

He said it in such an apologetic tone and with just the right delivery that Cain almost groaned. But at least Petra didn't appear to be taken in by it.

"And why would she do that?" she said, shaking her head. "My sister was not suicidal."

"But you didn't know her at the end, did you?" he said ever-so-gently. "She was not a happy person. We fought constantly. She wanted to get back together again, but I hadn't been with her for a long time, and that wasn't what I wanted for my world anymore," he said. "She was really fairly unstable."

"In what way?" she asked.

"Everything. Ever since she aborted her child, she was wrought with guilt and felt terrible. In fact, she even wanted me to get her pregnant again."

"So, it was your child she aborted in the first place," Pet-ra said. "That would make sense in her mind potentially. But, no, I don't believe she killed herself."

"And why is that?"

"Because she wasn't suicidal. That isn't who she was."

"And like I said, you didn't know her then."

She said, "But the idea of suicide still doesn't sit well."

"You're already dealing with the loss," he said. "Give it a couple weeks and then maybe some of this will make some sense." He smiled at her. "I know she didn't want to see you when she came into town the last time." He was twisting the knife that he had driven in earlier. "She was so depressed and figured you wouldn't want to see her because she'd had the abortion. I think, in her mind, she was thinking, if she got pregnant again, she could contact you, and the two of you could make up."

"I highly doubt she even thought that long and hard about how to fix our relationship," she said. "And, when we parted, it wasn't that bad."

"But she also wasn't very sound mentally, so her state of mind was anything but normal." He looked at the two men and said, "And since you won't spend some time with me, so I can share with you her last moments, or at least in the days and weeks beforehand," he quickly stumbled back from his mistake, "I'll leave you for another time." He looked back at Cain. "Since you're so good at staying alive, good luck with that." Then he turned and walked away.

Cain heard her gasp, as she looked up at him. "Did he just threaten you?"

"Guys like that always threaten," Cain said absentmindedly. He closed the door slowly, turned to look back at Eton and said, "Well?"

"Hard to say," Eton said. "I've got some photos, and I've got voice recordings. But we don't really have too much to go on."

"What are you checking?" Petra asked, feeling like she'd come in the middle of the conversation.

"A couple phone messages were left on the phone of one of the guys who tried to kill us in the museum. I'm checking to see if it was Tristan's voice on the message."

"Ah, you're looking for that definitive link, that he ordered the killing?"

"That he ordered the attack, anyway," he said. "It's always a little hard to know at this point in time."

"Well, he definitely killed my sister. Now I feel a little

bad for blaming Chico for it."

"Well, the suicide angle is interesting," He looked at Cain. "Is it possible?"

"No," he said. "I wouldn't think so. Of course forensics will need to confirm if any GSR is on her hand and on her forehead, but, even then, the angle isn't something you would be particularly prone to do. Most people stick the gun in their mouth or at their temple, thinking that will do it. In this case, it was a nice rounded bullet hole in the center of her forehead, and I didn't see a gun."

"And, of course, the door being locked from the inside supports the suicide theory," Eton said, with a nod.

"Exactly. If truly a suicide, the gun would be nearby the body. We saw no obvious gun in sight, but we didn't look around long enough to rule it out either," Cain said.

"No, but one is needed in order to make that suicide theory stick," Eton said. "So, provided enough goop and tissue were found in the barrel of the weapon," he said, "I'm quite sure that the police will have found a weapon. That suicide will be the official statement."

"That's not fair," Petra cried out in outrage.

"Nothing's fair," Cain said. "Remember that."

"Once again, I'm not sure I like your perspective on life."

CHAPTER 11

P ETRA LOOKED AT Eton and said, "Now what do we
do?"

"Well, now that Tristan's openly here, we'll trail him to
see who he visits, so we can connect more dots."

"You don't want to have an official talk with him?"

"We'd love to," Cain said cheerfully. "But Tristan won't
talk. Not the truth anyway. He's got his story down, which is
why I'm pretty damn sure a gun will be found at the crime
scene. Your sister's death will be blamed on her, as a suicide,
or, if that fails, he'll pin it on his father."

"It's all complete bullshit though."

"Bullshit warms up and spreads," he said, "so just stick
with what you know your sister to have been like and don't
let his lies get in the way of your memory of her."

Petra walked over and sagged into a chair. "It's all just so
wrong," she whispered.

"We have an extra reason now to be even more cautious
with your safety."

"Why?"

"Because," Cain said, "with Tristan in town, we're all at
risk."

"You think he'll attack us?"

"Absolutely," Cain said. "I'm surprised he didn't kill me
and you immediately after he killed the neighbor cop." At

her gasp, Cain realized he was speaking largely out loud and not really for her benefit. "He probably didn't, hoping to set you and me up for the death of the cop, like with your sister's setup to blame someone else. Regardless he can't really leave us alive. We're already causing enough trouble right here," he said.

"Not to mention the other issues that brought us here," Cain continued. "We'll just be thorns in Tristan's side until something is done. And the fact of the matter is, if he did have something to do with the attempt on our lives in Perth, it'll also piss him off that we showed up right here, in his hometown, and are additionally putting pressure on this situation with your sister. That, as much as anything, is the reason he's bolted back home again. And very publicly too. He's not hiding now, not like he was earlier. He's sure to have seen a video of some kind, showing that we were here and how he needed to come take care of business. Even coming to your apartment was part of that deal. Anything to have me take the fall."

"He did a pretty good job checking around, didn't he?" Eton noted.

"Checking around what?" Petra asked.

ETON GOT UP just then. He smacked Cain lightly on the shoulder. "I'll be back." And he walked out, closing the door behind him.

She looked at Cain. He looked at her but didn't say anything. She frowned. "Where's he going?"

"He'll go see where your friend just went to."

"Well, he's already gone, so that won't help much," she said.

"Not quite," he said. "I managed to slip a tracker into his pocket."

She stopped and stared at him. "You what?"

He shrugged. "Sorry if you don't like my methods," he said, "but we have to get to the end of this."

"I didn't even see you do that," she said in shock.

"That's the whole idea," he said, with a big smile. "You weren't supposed to see me do anything. Hopefully he didn't either."

CHAPTER 12

PETRA WALKED TO the kitchen and sat down by the window. "What will we do now? Just sit here?"

"Unless you can think of anybody in town who can help us?"

"What are you trying to find?" she asked. "I don't think what you're looking for is the same thing as what I'm looking for."

"You're looking for justice for your sister. I'm looking for justice for my dead friend."

She winced at that. "Sorry. I keep forgetting you've already lost somebody and had two other friends get hurt."

"It's not something I will ever forget," he said, "and these guys are still coming after us."

"You think Tristan's setting up to come after you now?"

"Why? Don't you?"

"Potentially," she said. "But I also hope more than a few answers are coming our way."

He nodded. "What about other friends of Tristan's?"

"No clue," she said. "He's not somebody I've ever wanted to spend time around."

"With good reason," he said. "And what about his comment that your sister was depressed?"

"How would I know? It's not like I had any kind of real communication with her after she left. I tried, but she up

139

and disappeared, until we found her yesterday," she said, her voice getting fainter. She gave her head a hard shake. "It's just so beyond anything I could have imagined."

"Maybe you can contact the police and see if there was any sign of a weapon with her."

He hadn't even finished speaking, when she already had her phone out. She waited until the detective answered her call. As soon as she heard his voice, she asked him flat-out, "Detective, was a weapon found with my sister? Was it a murder or are you considering suicide?"

"I don't have details to give you at this point."

"Why not?" she asked in exasperation. "Surely it's not that hard to tell me if a weapon was found. It's a yes or no question."

"A weapon was found," he confirmed. "But what I can't say is whether she fired it yet."

"So, at this point it could be either."

"Exactly. I promise we'll get you some information, as soon as we have some to share."

"Well, somehow I doubt you'll share too openly," she said. "And it's a little hard to sit around here waiting for answers, especially now that Tristan's back."

"What do you mean, Tristan's back?" he asked.

"Tristan just knocked on my apartment door and said that he knew nothing about my sister's death, but he understood that she committed suicide and that, if it wasn't, it must have been his father."

"How long ago did you see him?" he said, his voice all business.

"Maybe twenty minutes ago," she said. "You didn't know?"

"No," he said. "How would we? He's been out of town

for a long time."

"Well, he's not now," she said. "And I sure as hell would like to know what he's up to."

"You and me both," he said. "We'll pull him in and talk to him." With that, he hung up.

She frowned and looked at the phone. "He seemed actually surprised that Tristan was here."

"Well, it's great timing in terms of them having somebody to talk to who's a potential suspect," he said. "It's shitty timing if Tristan can somehow 'prove' he wasn't here earlier, shooting his neighbor cop, which of course you know he'll do."

"Right. If nothing else," she said, "he can always get your surveillance feed subpoenaed." He broke out laughing at that. She just glared at him. "I also have to deal with my father."

"You're getting a tox screen done," he said. "What else would you like to do?"

"I don't know. Maybe talk to my aunt?"

"Will that help?"

"No, probably not," she said. "But it might make me feel better."

"Then let's go," he said. "Absolutely no reason not to."

"Says you," she said, with half a smile.

As they stood, he said, "If nothing else, the walk will do you some good."

"And what about Eton?"

"Eton will let me know if he finds anything."

"Fine," she said, "let's go then."

As soon as they were outside, she looked around. "It's such a weird feeling to think that everybody's gone."

"Well, not quite everybody," he said.

"No, not everyone. It just seems like everyone," she said sadly.

He reached out and laced his fingers with hers. "Just stay positive."

"I'm trying," she said. "It's ... so frustrating."

"I know," he said.

As they walked down the street toward her aunt's place, she looked at him. "I thought you were leaving today."

"Change of plans," he said easily. "Tristan's shown up here, so we don't have to go hunting him down somewhere else."

"Was that where you were heading?"

"Yep, until he went on the move. Perfect for us."

"You know he's probably just here to take you out, right?"

"Yep, that's what we figured," he said.

"So are we safe to walk around so openly?"

Cain chuckled, nodded. "You bet. We've got eyes on us at all times." He pointed upward and all around as well.

She looked around suspiciously. "Is this a setup?"

"In what way?" he asked.

Such innocence was in his voice that she sighed. "Are you setting this up for him to attack us while we're out on a walk?"

"Hell, no!" he said. "I wouldn't take a chance with your life like that."

She wasn't sure she believed him or not. "I think you would do whatever you need to do to further your objectives," she murmured.

"Not at the risk of your life," he said in a reassuring manner.

"Well, I hope not," she said. "Enough shit has been going down around here lately."

"Another reason why we need to talk to your aunt."

"I doubt she'll have anything to say," she said.

"You might be surprised," he answered.

She shrugged. "My aunt and I have never gotten along."

"It sounds like some really old history is there."

"Very," she said. "But it's over now, just like so much else."

"You can still have a relationship with them, if you want to," he said. "Just because your father has passed on doesn't mean that you have to walk away from them too."

"I highly suspect there is nothing to walk away from," she murmured.

"And that would be sad, but it's possible," he said.

"They're up here," she said, as they went down a side street.

"Is this a different way?" he asked.

"Not quite," she said, "just another entrance into the back of the house."

"And you want to take the back road, why?"

"I can't really explain it," she said, "but my instincts are telling me to go that way."

"Well, the one thing that me and my team have always learned to trust is our instincts."

She shook her head. "My instincts aren't yours though."

"No, maybe not, but you'd be surprised at what we learn and understand about ourselves from something like this."

As they walked up to the house from the back alley, she opened the gate, and they stepped into the backyard. Inside the house a fight was going on, and things sounded pretty tense. Petra stopped in place, looked at him, and said, "Obviously this isn't a good time."

"Is there ever a good time?" he asked.

"No, of course not." But then she hesitated.

"Do you want to do something or not?"

She shrugged. "Well, we need answers."

"We do," he said, with a light laugh.

She frowned. "I still don't think they'll help much."

As they walked to the house, she heard the conversation better. "It's about money."

"That seems to be one of the biggest problems in their world." As they got closer, he pulled her against one of the big vine-covered arbors that they had dotting the area.

"What are you doing?" she whispered.

"Something weird is going on," he said.

She looked at him and said, "You mean, weirder than normal?"

He smiled down at her. "Absolutely weirder than normal." And she waited for him to let her go.

But he was hell-bent on holding her tight. Finally he said, "Can you hear the conversation?"

She nodded. "But I'm not listening to it."

"Listen to it," he said, his voice hard. "I'm not completely versed in this dialect."

She listened, her eyes closed, and then she stiffened. "They're talking about my father and his money," she murmured.

He nodded. "That's what I heard too."

She strained her ears.

Her aunt screamed at her uncle, "We needed the money."

"We got paid," he said, snapping back at his wife. Petra didn't think she'd ever heard her uncle talk like that to Migi.

"But we don't have enough. It's not enough. We need

more," Migi shouted.

"Then you know what the answer is," her uncle snapped at her again.

"I should never have married you," she roared.

"No, you shouldn't have," he said, "and I shouldn't have married you either. We've had this argument over and over again though," he said, "and it won't change anything now."

"We need money," she said, "so we have to make decisions."

"What decision do you want to make?" he asked.

"She has to go," she said.

"You're the one who wanted me to take care of her father, and I was happy to leave him as he was."

"Sure, cleaning his butt every day," she sneered. "That's hardly the life for us."

"Maybe not," he said, "but it kept us in food."

"But then you killed him for money, but where is it?" she snapped.

"Well, I was supposed to get paid more than what I got from him. What am I supposed to do now?"

"You let him cheat you out of it," she snapped. "Go and get the rest of the money."

"He told me that he'd kill me if I came back for more."

"Sure he did," she snapped. She stared out the window, and Cain and Petra saw Migi pointing outside. "We should never have sold off the land."

"What could we have done though?" her uncle said sadly.

"We should have just hired workers," she murmured. "It would have been tough for a year, but that would have been all. Now we keep selling off our assets, and we have nothing left."

"And, once again," he said, "there are still very few answers for us right now."

"You were supposed to get all the money. I told you."

"He said he didn't have it. Then, because I kept pushing him, he said he'd kill me if I came back."

Petra started at that.

"I highly doubt it. Since when did you ever push for anything?"

Such a sneering tone was in her aunt's voice that Petra winced for her uncle, even though the conversation was just too hard to believe. She was still stuck on the fact that they were talking about having killed her father, and she didn't even know how that could be. It was all so wrong on so many levels.

As she stood here, locked in Cain's arms, she listened for more, but the conversation moved to the front of the house.

Finally he spoke up. "Did I hear what I thought I heard?"

Tears dotted her eyes, and she nodded. "They were paid to kill my father."

"And your uncle didn't get all the money, right?"

She nodded. "No, apparently not. She was bitter at that too. He wasn't even worth paying the full price for. Because they had no recourse, they'd already done the deed and now they shared the guilt." She rested her head against Cain's chest. "It's still all so wrong," she whispered. "I don't understand it."

"We'll get there," he said, "and they will pay."

She murmured, as she shook her head. "Nobody's paid for anything yet," she said, "except me."

"Hold that thought," he said. "We will get justice for your father. And your sister."

Just then the kitchen door slammed open, hard.

Cain immediately pulled her back tight and whispered against her ear, "Is there any way to get out of here, so we're not seen?"

She looked up at him, her eyes wide, as she considered the backyard, and then she shook her head. "No. They'll come right by here," she whispered. "We have to get out of here and fast."

He leaned down and whispered into her ear, "Too late. Your uncle's already outside." And she froze in his arms.

CAIN HELD PETRA close, as her uncle stormed past them. Cain pulled her just far enough around the trellis that they were hidden against the fence and behind the greenery. Her uncle would have to turn and actually look hard to see them. Cain studied the fence behind him, wondering if he could pick her up and toss her over the side, so at least Petra would not be in danger. It was one thing to suspect the aunt and uncle of murder; it was another thing to have confirmation.

With one kill under their belt, it wasn't hard for them to consider a second one, especially if it would save their assets. And, in this case, they might even get a bonus for it. Although payment and collection were apparently a problem. The uncle stormed into the back alleyway, and Cain whispered, "We'll give him a minute, then we'll head out and turn around, as if we're coming in from the alleyway again."

She looked up, still dazed, but she nodded. He gave it a count check to the kitchen and then quickly raced her to the gate that had bounced closed after the uncle went through. As he pushed it open, he saw the uncle at the far end of the alleyway, so he walked around the house and came up through the neighbor's yard and went to the front yard and then approached.

"Change of plans?"

"Your uncle was out there."

She nodded. "He tends to spend a fair amount of time storming up and down the back alley."

"Probably the only way he survived living with your aunt all this time."

"But apparently not my father," she said bitterly.

"You know that this does give credence to your fear that they might have done something to him, debilitating him in the first place."

She hunched her shoulders at that. "I just want to kill them both," she whispered.

"That won't help," he said, "but I understand the sentiment."

"What is it with the people in this town?" she asked.

"When you end up with something like this—a town that is sinking, with really depressed economics, you find people get desperate," he said. "Some towns pull together and help each other. In this case it seems to be an issue of annihilating the competition."

She was bitter about that too. But he squeezed her hand, pulled her forward, and said, "Listen. We need to talk to your aunt right now. She's pretty upset and a little on the wild side, so who knows what she might let out."

Cain walked Petra around to the front, and they intentionally made a lot of noise. They stomped on the front step as they headed to the front door. As she opened the door, she called out to her aunt. Migi answered from the back, in the kitchen. As they came around the corner, they found her aunt, sitting at the table, glaring at them.

Petra frowned. "I just wanted to talk to you about Papa," she said.

The aunt just shrugged. "I don't give a shit," she said. "I cleaned that old man's butt for a long enough."

Petra stiffened beside her.

"He was the same age as you," she said, with difficulty. "But if that's how you felt about my father, I'm surprised you looked after him all this time."

"I needed the money," she said. "It's not just the invalids who have to eat, you know."

"I'm sorry," she said. "I didn't realize things were that difficult."

"You knew," she said. "You just didn't give a shit."

"And, if I supposedly knew, what was I supposed to do about it?" Petra asked incredulously. "You've got your house and property. I don't have anything like that."

"Well, you do now," she said. "Your father's property will go to you."

"Yeah," she replied, remembering how Cain had suggested she play it. "But it's already been sold to pay you to look after him," she said. "I don't have much left."

"Are you sure?" her aunt asked shrewdly. "I think you're lying."

"Why would I lie?" she said.

"So that you don't have to share what you have with us, of course. Do you know how hard it has been for us? How much of our time and effort went into looking after your father? The least you could do is share."

Cain watched, as she swallowed hard.

"I did share," she said. "I gave you a job ... to look after him."

Cain saw Petra struggle with the words wanting to escape her tight control.

Her aunt just snorted. "You have more than that because your father had more than that."

"But what money is left is for my future."

"I knew it," she sneered. "You don't care about us. You don't care about anything but yourself. We took your father in, when nobody else would. You couldn't even afford to look after him, and then you sold the property. But you didn't share it with us, did you? Now you'll get his full estate, and still, we get nothing."

Petra recoiled at the very selfish and vindictive words coming from her aunt's mouth. "I guess this isn't a good time to talk to you," she said, with difficulty. Then she turned to Cain. "I'd like to go now," she murmured.

He hesitated, other questions to ask the aunt burning in the back of his mind, but he nodded and said, "That's a good idea."

Her peace of mind was so much more important than anything this old bat might have to say. He held out his hand, and she immediately slipped hers into it; then he tugged her toward the front door.

"Yeah, disappear with your little sleazy friend there," she said, "like that'll help."

"I don't know what you mean," he said and turned to look at her. "Nor do I understand why you called me that."

"We've heard you're here hunting down some of the locals," she said. "How is that a normal thing? We heard all about it. You come in here, using my place to hunt down our local people," she sneered. "You're nothing but a hired gun."

He stared at her, feigning shock.

She shook her shoulders. "You think we're just all backward old folks here," she said. "We know how this works."

"How what works?"

"You come in here, take out a bunch of people who matter to us, drive the economy down even lower, then buy up property at bargain prices, only to demolish everything and to put up a big development."

"That's the gossip?" He stared at her, not understanding how any of these pieces fit together.

"Where did you hear all that from?" Petra asked.

She shrugged. "Tristan, I suppose. He's not a bad kid," she said.

"Well, except for when he doesn't pay his bills fully, right?" Petra said.

Instantly her aunt stiffened. "What are you talking about?"

"You know exactly what I'm talking about," she said, "but that's all right. You'll get everything that's coming to you."

And, with that, Cain ushered her out the front door. As soon as they got outside, he asked, "Was that necessary?"

"Maybe not," she said, "but it definitely felt better than anything else I said."

He nodded and smiled at that. "I get it," he said. "I really do. But pulling the tiger by the tail isn't what we need right now."

"She killed my father," she said. "Anything we do that hurts her is good."

"Do you know of any cops we can trust?"

"I don't know anybody here in law enforcement," she said. "It's a small town, but the police change all the time."

"In that case, I'll have to get somebody to help us out,"

he said.

"Local?"

"No, not local," he said. "I'm calling Ice."

As soon as he had Ice on the phone, he quickly explained what they'd overheard.

"Wow. Nice place you're at," she said on the phone.

"No, not nice at all. We're talking some seriously ugly people here, some with a sense of entitlement that is just unbelievable."

"Right. Expect a phone call in a little bit."

"Will do." When he hung up, he said, "She's contacting some of her people."

"I want to be Ice," she said. "I want to have people."

He laughed. "Other people are out there, like her, but not too many," he said. "She's in a class of her own. She's helping us search for our friend, but we fear he is already dead, as well as hunt those who are trying to kill the rest of us." He needed to remember to ask for any updates on Bullard. And Terkel. Cain hated to admit it, but he was desperate to believe Bullard was alive. And needed Terk to give Cain that bit of hope.

Just then he got a phone call. He looked down to see it was Ryland. "Hey, anything new on that satellite you're monitoring for us?"

"He's at his father's house," he said. "You might want to head that way."

"Anything interesting?"

"Yeah," he said. "I lost track of Eton."

CHAPTER 13

WHEN CAIN TURNED and looked down the street, everything inside him went hard and craggy looking.

Petra had heard just enough of that conversation to immediately say, "You're not going without me."

He frowned and slid her a sideways glance.

She shook her head. "No. I don't know what's going on, but, if Eton needs help, he needs both of us."

He gave her a half smile. "It's not your kind of work, sweetie."

"It doesn't matter," she said. "There will be something I can do to help out."

"I love the sentiment," he said, "but the reality is that you'll be in the way, and my attention will be diverted, trying to look after you, while I'm trying to find out what's going on with Eton."

"Let's go take a look." This time her hand squeezed his. "Come on. Stand strong," she said.

He smiled and said, "You have no idea what may happen."

"No, I don't," she admitted. "I get that this is the stuff you do, and it's dangerous all the time," she said, "but we have a lot at play here."

"I'm not planning on blowing anything," he said, "except maybe the guy's head off, if he hurt Eton."

"And that's what Tristan wants to do?"

"Tristan wants to kill Eton," he said. "Tristan's part of the same team who took down some of my crew."

"So, we won't give him that chance."

Cain stopped in the middle of the street, as a car crept up and went around them.

Petra thought she saw Cain give an imperceptible nod to the driver.

"You don't have a stake in this," Cain said to Petra.

"You're wrong, Cain. I threw my lot in with you, and now you have it, whether you like it or not," she said defiantly. "Come on. We're wasting time."

"I can hardly just walk down there and expect a welcome."

"That's exactly what you'll get," she said, "because that's the kind of scumbag he is."

"What are you expecting him to do?" he asked, interested in the sudden change in her.

"Well, the sneaky part of him would just shoot you from the window, if he got the chance," she said. "Unfortunately he has threatened so many people in town that everyone will turn a blind eye and just be grateful that it doesn't involve them. They'll just want you to leave, so it will all be over, so things can go back to normal."

He stared at her thoughtfully. "That's a good point," he said. "I suppose now some might want you gone as well, right?"

"Well, my aunt and uncle want me gone obviously. And, if they could manage to kill me and collect, while all this is going on, they wouldn't be so upset about not getting the rest of their payment from Tristan."

"Maybe that's precisely what he promised."

"Nothing would surprise me at this point," she said, her voice cracking slightly. "We can't let people like this go on unchecked."

"I gather the four founding families have always been a bit of a law unto themselves?"

"Always," she confirmed. "Nothing nice about either of the families in this mess."

"What about the rest of the town?"

"Most of the good guys left," she said. "And the old ones? Well, I don't think they have any family left. It's a hard road when it's only you against the rest."

"Nobody needs that," he agreed. "But I won't stand here and let him take out my friend."

"Of course not," she said, "and that's what Tristan's expecting."

"Exactly. So now we have to get in there and surprise him," he said.

"In that case, we need to get moving now." She headed out, leading him through another alleyway.

"Where are we going?" he protested.

"Just a different entrance."

"Is this whole place full of these secret routes?"

"Little side streets, yes, because all of these were, at one time, one really big property," she said. "Then parts were sold off, but people kept bits and pieces."

"Strange town."

"A town of strong loyalties," she said. "When they hate, they hate deep. When they love, it's the same."

"But the veil between love and hate—it's very thin," he warned her.

"Yeah, I found that out. I had no idea my aunt and uncle were the people they are," she said. "It's a bit of a shock."

"But you're handling it well," he said.

"I'm not actually. I'm really not. I'm just holding on to get justice."

"Well, Ice has got something going."

"How about calling for backup right now?"

"Not until I know what's going on."

"And your friends are tracking him?"

"Well, they've tracked him to the house."

"Nobody should even be there because of the murder scene," she said. "My sister's body has barely been taken away. Shouldn't the forensics people still be there?"

"No, they're probably done by now," he said. "I mean, it takes time but usually not that long. They should have been done sometime during the night, I would think."

She nodded. "I hope they actually gave it some thought, instead of just writing it off as a quick suicide."

"I don't think they would have done that," he said. "If nothing else, they have to show proof to their supervisors to get it signed off."

She gave a laugh. "I don't know if it's still the same police chief because I don't keep up with that, but it used to be the old drunk's brother."

At that, Cain stopped, looked at her, and said, "Seriously?"

She nodded.

"Then we won't see any kind of justice from that group, will we?"

"No." Her voice was thick with emotion. "We won't."

"Then we'll have to do it another way," he said, with a half smile.

"I hope you have some miraculous way to make it happen," she said, "because I don't."

"I do, and her name is Ice."

As they stepped along the fence, he pulled out his phone and quickly sent a message to both Ryland and Ice.

"Who's this guy Ryland you were talking to?"

"One of the ones who got hurt in the last attack," he said. "All because of Tristan's orders, it appears."

"I still don't understand why they went after you."

"That's what I'm hoping to find out."

"Tristan's not likely to talk, even if you do get a hold of him," she murmured. "And, even if he does, you can't believe anything that comes out of his mouth."

"Nice people you got here."

"Desperate people," she said. "Like you said earlier, they just want to live their lives in some sort of peace and quiet."

"That may be," he said, "but their town is about to get blown wide open. And, if the police chief doesn't do his job properly, he won't be around to do it again."

"It'll take more than you to put him out of office," she said.

"Depends on how much he's guilty of," he murmured.

They were up against the house already. She stared at the huge property, the stone walls, and the big house where her sister's life had ended. "You know what? I'd really like to go in with guns blazing, just shooting up everything," she said. "The trouble is, we'd likely kill the wrong people, and the right people will continue to live a nice cozy life, like they always seem to."

"Now follow my lead. Don't talk. We'll go do some surveillance. See what we've got."

Cain approached the house from the back, his phone in his hand. She watched as he made a connection with somebody. She wanted to ask questions, but he'd been very clear about not making a sound. He looked down at the phone and frowned.

She put her hands on her hips and glared at him.

He looked toward the house, then leaned forward and whispered in her ear, "I want you to stay right here, and, if anything happens to me, I want you to text this number." Quickly he sent a number to her phone.

When her phone vibrated, she looked at it and asked, "And who is this?"

"Ice."

She nodded. "How will I know if anything happened to you?"

"If I don't come back out within a few minutes," he said, "and you hear gunshots."

"Are you telling me to call her if I hear anything?"

"Only if it sounds like something I can't get out of." He hesitated, then said, "That's very nebulous, I know."

"Just go," she said. "I'll figure it out."

He smiled, then leaned over and kissed her gently. "Thank you."

She reached out and placed a finger on his lips and said, "Come back."

"I will," he said.

"Promise?"

"Promise," he said, adding a smile, and, with that, he was gone.

CAIN SHOULDN'T HAVE made a promise like that because this was life and death right now. And, if somebody up there had hurt Eton, there would be hell to pay, and, before Cain died, he would make sure that somebody else paid first. In order to make that happen, he had to get into position, so he needed to get on it.

He moved swiftly alongside the house, checking doors and windows. So far, nothing would let him inside without going around to the front door. He kept avoiding that because, chances were, that's where Tristan was watching. Any smart team would be watching the entire place, but he also figured they would let Cain get inside to a certain degree, then close whatever trap they had. He just wanted to make sure he had a better end game than that.

Finally, at the back, he found a small cracked window. It was barely big enough for him to get in. He removed the pieces of glass quietly and slipped inside. As he landed, he turned to look back through the window and saw her watching him from under the canopy of a huge olive tree. He gave her a thumbs-up and disappeared inside. It felt odd to leave her there, like she was watching his back.

But this was different. It wasn't the same as a team member, but somebody was watching him for a completely different reason. He shook his head, trying to throw off the attachment that grew between them—at least for the present.

He needed to focus right now. Eton was his concern and Tristan, the bastard who'd killed her sister. Cain had no doubt in his mind that Tristan had done that. Cain didn't know how he'd managed to get out of the room without unlocking the doors, but he knew Tristan had found a way somehow. Now that Cain was in the basement of the house, he crept through the darkness, wondering just what the hell was down here. As he turned on the flashlight of his phone, he saw weapons. Cases and cases of weapons.

He let out a silent whistle and quickly took photos, sending them off to Ice and Ryland. Somebody needed to ensure this arsenal was collected and not handed out to the next group of criminals. Cain was hoping for documentation on some of it, and, if they got a chance, they'd get back down here. But that wasn't the priority right now. He had one thing on his mind, and that was making sure Eton was okay.

After searching all the rooms in the basement and not finding his friend, he moved to the main floor. No way to know where Tristan was within the property. But, in a quirky moment, Cain figured that Tristan was probably either up in his father's room or where Petra's sister had died, although that wouldn't be anything more than a morbid thought. Surely nobody wanted to stay in that room.

This guy was sick and a bastard, so maybe he would stay in that room.

As Cain crept through this level, he found absolutely no sign of anyone. He didn't know what happened to the drunk father either. As Cain headed down and around what appeared to be an office, he slowed his steps as he saw someone through one of the sheer Gloucester panels on the French doors, separating the office from the rest of the floor. He crept up slowly but didn't recognize who it was. The chair was turned around, facing the window, as if he were lost in thought. But as Cain got closer, he winced because the person wasn't lost in thought. He was lost to the world.

He knew as he arrived, it would be the father. Cain crept in and took a look, only to see that the old man had a bullet in his forehead. He had a gun in his hand, but it was a long shotgun. It wasn't the one Morgan had used to shoot at them earlier, before they'd found Petra's sister, nor was it one he had used to kill himself. To have done it himself would have taken a handgun; that shotgun could not have done the job. He suspected Tristan was the killer once again. But Cain still saw no sign of him right now. He was somewhere in this house, and Cain had to find him—before the tables were turned.

He slipped from the room and made it to the hallway, when he heard footsteps on the stairs. Swearing silently, he disappeared down the hallway to where he thought he could stay under cover and out of sight.

Tristan walked into the office, snorting at the old man. "Son of a bitch wasn't good for anything anyway," he muttered. He opened a bunch of drawers, taking stuff out, but Cain couldn't see what it was. He just heard the sounds of things being removed and slapped down on top of the desk.

"All you had to do was keep that damn journal safe. That's all we asked of you," he muttered. "You could have kept the house. You could have kept everything. It's not like anybody wants to live in this godforsaken town anyway."

Cain crept up closer, only to see that Tristan had two handguns placed on the desk.

"He'll be here any minute, you know? I want some of this paperwork upstairs, so I can talk to him. And I've got to get rid of the one guy first."

He talked in a conversational tone, as if his father were sitting there, listening to him. His father was a long time away from listening to him.

"What the hell did you do with that shit anyway? I've been looking everywhere for it. Be typical of you to go hide it, just to make my life fucking difficult," he snapped in an ugly tone. "If you weren't dead, I'd fucking kill you again right now. Where the hell did you put it?" And then he straightened and said, "I don't have time for this right now."

He stormed from the office and headed back upstairs. As he was halfway up the stairs, he stopped at the landing and looked out through the window. "Still not here. Fucking asshole, nobody can ever get here on time either."

Unsure who Tristan was talking about, whether Cain or somebody else that Tristan was looking for, Cain stayed very still. As soon as Tristan was upstairs, Cain listened to hear the sound of his footsteps going down the hallway.

Cain hopped up on the railing and went up, hand over hand, foot over foot. He moved up without touching any of the stairs that squeaked, knowing that would alert the man that a predator was on the way.

Once he was upstairs, he hopped off the railing silently, then slipped into the same bedroom where Petra's sister had been killed. He stood here for a long moment, looked around, then walked to the closet where the weapons had been kept in the room, hoping that Tristan had left it all here and that the cops hadn't found the true stash. They should have, but he opened the doors and smiled because it was all still here. They had removed the weapons in the front section but hadn't found the false walls, revealing the real arsenal.

He quickly snatched two handguns, checked them, and almost purred with joy when he found they were fully loaded. He stuck one in his belt in back and took the other one in his hand, then picked up a small one and slipped it into his boot.

Just then, he heard yelling at the other end of the hallway. He listened, wondering if the expected company had arrived. He walked to the doorway, his ear against the slightly open door to hear Tristan yelling at someone.

"You were supposed to be here twenty minutes ago," he

said. "You know I'll get set up over this. No way I'm going down without taking you with me."

Cain listened and thought about the implications of his words. Tristan most likely expected somebody to come help him deal with Cain and Eton.

As Cain listened, Tristan was once again yelling. "I'll just kill this one," he said, "then I don't have to worry about him. If you won't be here to give me a hand, then I don't need you either," he said. Hearing no audible response, Cain assumed Tristan was talking on the phone.

Taking the chance, he moved forward a little into the hallway. Just then he heard footsteps coming up the front porch and the front door opening. He dashed into the large bathroom on the side and listened as somebody talking into a phone raced up the stairs.

"I'm right fucking here. I told you that I was coming."

Cain looked out, and, sure enough, it was Petra's uncle. Cain stared in surprise, wondering when the hell this sudden change was done to the equation.

Just then the door at the other end opened, and Tristan said, "There you are. I told you that you're only getting paid if you help me get through this."

"You should have gotten some of your other guys," he said. "This isn't my field."

"I don't give a shit if it's your field or not," he snapped. "Did you bring some weapons?"

"I don't do weapons. I told you that," Pedro said in whining tones.

"Right," he said. "Why am I not surprised? Well, you better stand watch at the front and let me know if he comes."

"We saw them this morning," he said.

"When?"

"They came to talk to my wife."

He snorted. "Why would anybody want to talk to her?" He sneered. "Talk about a major loser."

"It doesn't matter," he said. "It's the same answer as always. She is my wife."

"It's ridiculous, Pedro," he said. "You should have taken my father's offer a long time ago and deep-sixed that witch."

"I couldn't," he said.

"Whatever. Finish this job with me, and then you'll get paid."

"That's what you said last time. She told me that I shouldn't do any more work for you until you paid me for the last job."

"You should be paying me for helping you take out your brother-in-law," he said. "You've been wanting to do that forever."

"But we couldn't because we needed the money he got us monthly. Besides, you were supposed to pay us enough that we didn't have to kill him."

"Whatever," he said. "That wife of yours can't live within her means, no matter how much it is. You would have been better off getting rid of her a long time ago."

"I loved her."

"Well, you don't now," he said. "After you get the money, you better go take her out too. It's the only way you'll ever be free."

"I know," he said, "but I can't let her know that."

"Nope. You can even have the house and everything you want here. It'll be a mess to clean up but—"

"You're always talking like that," he cut in, "but I never actually get anything."

"That's not my fault," he said. "Blame that on your useless wife. Get rid of her and then ..."

There was more talk, but it was in low tones, and Cain couldn't make out all the words.

Cain had listened, shocked as they made arrangements to first kill Eton, then deal with Cain, and finally take out Migi, Pedro's own wife.

So much for love. Cain might understand the sentiment, given the woman involved, but it was hardly the way to go. And now he had an extra person to deal with, though Cain didn't know just what kind of an element the uncle would be in this scenario. Pedro had already fooled Cain once. The last thing he wanted to do was get fooled a second time. But now he was up against Tristan too. Normally that wasn't an issue, but he had to shake him out of the room in order to access him.

"Go, go, go," Tristan said. "Get down there and watch that front door."

Cain waited as the footsteps of the uncle went down past the doorway Cain was behind. He poked his head out to check, but the door of the room Tristan was in was nearly closed. Cain silently walked up behind the uncle, immediately snapped an arm around his neck in a chokehold, slapped a hand over his mouth, dragging him into the bedroom where the girl had been shot.

There he knocked him out and quickly grabbed handcuffs from the weapons room. Soon he had the man tied up, a bandanna stuffed in his mouth, and, shoving him under the bed, left him there. Cain briefly wondered what kind of mess might be under that bed, but he wasn't too bothered because, of all the things in life that he cared about, this guy was not it. But he didn't want to kill him either, figuring Petra would want justice first.

And then, with that, Cain stepped out and slowly made his way along the hallway to the end. As soon as he got up to the almost closed door, he listened intently, but there was not a sound. So, either Tristan was waiting for him to make a move, or he was just sitting there, pondering life. Ignoring the asshole was hard to do.

Cain knew he just had to time his approach to make sure he had the element of surprise.

A phone rang inside, and he hoped it was Tristan's and not Eton's. Tristan answered it. Only hearing half of the conversation still gave Cain enough to sort it out.

"I know," he said. "It'll be over in ten minutes."

"Yeah, yeah, I know. I'll take out the old man too. And leave the aunt. I'll do that on my own," he said. "That woman is a fucking bitch." He paused. "Half an hour out, bring the wheels around. I want to get out of this shithole and the sooner, the better." Again he stopped to hear the person on the other end. "No, I've got one. I haven't seen the other one yet. He's on his way, I'm sure."

Tristan groaned. "I told you that I've got it handled. You can always count on me. You know that. We got a bunch of them. Chico took care of a couple them, including Bullard. I've got the two here. We'll take them out," he said. "Then it's to you." Tristan went silent again, listening to his caller.

"You taking out the next ones on your own? Or have you got somebody to do a hit-and-run?" he asked. "Sorry, not my business, I get it. Not my problem either. This is what I agreed to do. The money's already been transferred, right?"

CHAPTER 14

PETRA HUNKERED DOWN low under the trees and waited. Her heart slammed against her chest, and she just knew something was wrong. Besides the fact that Eton was in there. She thought she'd heard voices, but it was so damn hard to hear out here. It was another hot day, while evening approached. She was used to those, but it certainly wasn't something that she needed right now. She could almost feel beads of sweat rolling down her back, and she wasn't sure if that was nervous tension or just the weather.

She buried her face against her knees and wrapped her arms tightly around them, squeezing as hard as she could just to ease some of the tension. This was not where she expected to be at this point in her life. She had been so buried, trying to deal with her father and to keep up his care and, when she had free time, to work on whatever was going wrong in his system. She hadn't had a chance to look forward at all.

Her father had been young enough and could have gone on twenty years in that condition, until apparently her aunt and uncle had taken him out. And didn't that just set Petra's nerves on edge and bring up so many questions about their relationship. And about her mother. Did they have something to do with that death too? Petra really didn't want to think it, but, if they had done this much, why wouldn't they? They could have caused the fire that killed her grandparents as well, plus killed her mother and now her father. And Cain was right. If they'd already killed once, or potentially two or three times, taking Petra out wouldn't be a big issue at all. And, if Chico and Tristan had anything to do with this nightmare, well, anything was possible.

Petra lifted her head and looked around. She thought she heard something, but, under this olive tree, she was really struggling to hear anything. And it seemed like a great place to hide, but, at the same time, it distorted the sounds— noises that were particularly disruptive to her peace of mind. The last thing she needed was to get caught, just adding to the complications that Cain was no doubt dealing with.

The minute she thought about that, she wondered if she should get out of here. He had told her to hunker down and to stay hidden, but she felt something odd. She twisted suddenly, looking behind her, and almost cried out when she saw the handgun pointing directly at her. She threw herself off to the side, when feminine laughter rolled over her.

"Do you really think you'll avoid a bullet just by dodging it?" Her aunt sneered. "Get out of there," she said. "I want you to stand up and face me, when I pull this trigger."

Not knowing what else to do, Petra slowly pulled herself up from the undergrowth of the trees and stared in shock at her aunt. "Why?" she asked. "What is this all about?"

"We're just done," her aunt said, with a hard shrug. "We're so done. With you, your family, the whole mess. Even after everything we've done, you will still end up with all the money."

"What money?" she asked.

Migi just shook her head. "As if you don't know."

"I don't know very much, no, because none of this makes any sense."

"Our parents left everything to your mother, instead of sharing it with both daughters, and then your mother left everything to your father. Now, everything's been left to you. But I also know that, when you go, we're the last of the family," she said. "Now that your sister's dead of course. That was most convenient."

"Hardly convenient for her," Petra said, stiffening in outrage against her aunt. "So all of this—it's just about money?"

"Without money, there is nothing," she said. "Try not having any just once and see what it's like to put food on the table and to pay the bills."

"And yet you could have gotten jobs," she said.

"We tried," she said. "Do you think we didn't try? What do you think we are?"

She didn't even dare respond to that. "So you'll just shoot me right here?" she said. "Don't you think that'll be a little suspicious?"

"I doubt it," she said. "So much is going on right now already. Besides, Tristan's a piece of shit. He got my husband into so much trouble." She sneered. "Anything that makes trouble for him is perfect."

"Are you telling me my uncle was working for Tristan?" She gasped in horror, as her aunt remained silent. "Oh, my God, did he know about my sister?"

"No, neither of us knew about her," she said. "That's just disgusting. To think of that mouthy little brat's body up there, rotting away on the bedding like that, that's just gross."

Petra didn't know what to think about the words spewing from her aunt's mouth. So much disgust and hatred. "How long have you hated us?" she asked. "Forever?"

"Absolutely," she said. "I was engaged to your father, you know."

At that, Petra stopped, her hand going to her chest.

Her aunt nodded. "I was engaged to be married to him," she said, her voice swelling with fury. "Then my sister came home from overseas, where she'd been traveling with friends. She and your father took one look at each other, and that was it. *Love at first sight.*" She sniffed at that. "He broke up with me, hooked up with her, and they were married within sixty days. Sixty days!" she yelled.

"The only good thing was they didn't choose my same wedding day," she said, "but how do you think I felt, watching them year after year?" She continued, "When she finally died after giving birth, I was overjoyed. I figured he'd turn to me, and I could get rid of my husband at that point. But he didn't. Instead he did that 'there's only one love in my life forever' bullshit," she snapped. "And he would never have another relationship because of the memory of my perfect sister," she said. "I've hated all of you. But not him. I hate what he did to me, but I could never hate him."

Seeing the look on Petra's face, she continued, "When you love, you really love. At least I did. That he tossed my love in the dirt—not once, but twice—hurt me more than I could ever say. But, as much as I wanted to hate him, I never could."

"And yet you didn't want to look after him," Petra said quietly.

"No, of course not. I didn't want to see him like that. It hurt. And he was so pathetic. It was just impossible to deal with on a day-to-day basis. All I could think of was all the things that could have been."

"Wasn't it you who made him like that?" she asked quietly.

Her aunt stared at her in shock. "No," she said, "not at all."

"Are you sure? Didn't you try to poison him or give him something that caused him to have a heart attack in the kitchen that day?"

"No," she said, "that plate was for my husband. He was the one who was supposed to die."

"My God," Petra said, shaking her head and taking a half step back.

Her aunt waved the handgun in her direction. "But the idiot switched plates. He wasn't supposed to do that, but he did. I don't think he knew about it. He got a little bit of food poisoning from it, but your father took the brunt of it."

"Jesus," she whispered.

"Besides, your uncle has become useful in the last little bit."

"In what way?" Petra asked, with a nod toward the house. "This?"

"To a certain extent, yes," she said. "His jobs with Tristan have given us a little bit more money."

Everything the woman said seemed to be about money, and it was driving Petra crazy. "There's a lot more to life than money," she said quietly.

"You're young," her aunt replied. "You still believe in romance and happily ever after. It's all bullshit," she snapped. "I had it, and it was taken away."

"I'm sorry about that," Petra said, and she meant it because she couldn't imagine how that would have hurt and knew it had been eating at her aunt all these years. "I can only presume that my mother and father were deeply in love and that they couldn't see beyond that to anything else."

"No, they didn't care about anything," she said, and her features settled into the heavily wrinkled bitter woman who Petra knew. "But, for me, it was never the same. They were happy, and every day they were happy just hurt that much more. Even knowing she was pregnant with you made my life so much harder. And then, when I could never have children"—she shook her head—"that added insult to injury."

"I'm sorry about that too," she said. "I always wondered why you'd never had any."

"Because I couldn't," she said. "That's all there was to it. But I know that, if your father had been my husband, I would have had his babies."

"Maybe," she said, "or maybe you wouldn't. We don't know that."

"I know that her children were meant to be mine."

"And yet you hated me and my sister," she said.

"Because you weren't mine," she said. "And that makes all the difference."

"So now what?" Petra asked. "I can't imagine this ending in a good way for any of us."

"Well, not for you," she said. "As your only family member, I'll inherit." She sneered. "So, as far as I'm concerned, we don't need you anymore. And, once we have that money, I'll take care of that nuisance Pedro as well."

"Wow," Petra said, in a mocking tone, her mind searching for any way to get out of this. Her aunt might have a gun, but, short of her getting in a killing shot, surely Petra could overpower the much older woman. She wasn't sure that her aunt had experienced much defiance in her life, except when her father had broken up with her.

Maybe he'd been the smart one and had actually seen

something in her. Petra thought back in her history, wondering if there had been any sign that her father had been against her aunt, but it was never there. He always seemed to be welcome here, and they'd often commiserated and sat outside, spending many a happy evening together. So, had all this laid buried underneath them this whole time?

"When did all this surface?" she asked Migi. "I don't remember you having any arguments with my father, not even when I was a child."

"Of course not," she said. "And I wouldn't have, until he got hurt."

"By your hand," she said, "as you tried to murder your husband."

"Whatever," she said. "It didn't work."

"So, which of you killed my father?" she said.

"No one," the aunt said. "He was debilitated still, from the previous poisoning."

"I'm pretty sure my uncle is saying you did it," she said, frowning.

Her aunt stared at her in shock. "I did not," she said. "Remember that part about loving him?"

"Remember that saying about love and hate being two sides of a double-edged sword?"

Migi sneered. "But then you don't really understand what real love is anyway, do you?" she said. "You've never even had a boyfriend."

"I have so," she said.

Her aunt frowned. "I don't think you have," she said, instantly dismissing anything she said.

Petra stared at her and said, "What does any of that have to do with anything?"

"It doesn't," she said. "Nothing has anything to do with

you."

"Oh." Petra squeezed her eyes shut hard. Having lost control of the conversation, she could only wonder where her aunt's mental health had ended up. Obviously she was a very unhappy woman, but how far the poison had actually gone she could only imagine. "So? Now what?" she said, studying Migi's face and waiting for any sign that she would pull the trigger. "Is that good for you? You'll just stand out here in the open and shoot me?"

"Not quite," she said, looking around, as if for inspiration.

"You came here out of the blue with a gun?"

"Not quite," she said. "I followed my husband."

At that, Petra cocked her head and asked, "Where is he?"

"In the house. Tristan needed him for something."

"For what?" Petra asked, a horrible sinking feeling inside her heart.

"Doesn't matter," Migi said. "It's got nothing to do with you."

"You know you can't trust Tristan, right?"

"I know. He's already screwed us out of money, which is why we have to do this, so we can get the full amount he owes us."

"Why would he do that now?" Petra said. "He'll just kill you."

"Maybe not," she said. "Maybe we'll kill him first. Then we'll get his money and yours."

"Is there no end to the devious, crippled attitude in your head?" she asked. "Surely we deserve a little more than such callousness."

"You don't deserve anything," she said. "Nothing! Do you hear me?" She started to scream at her. "You're nothing but a loser! Just like your father."

"Right, my father, who you loved so much?"

But there was no talking to her. Apparently her aunt was well and truly heading down a pathway that didn't bode well for any of them. Petra took a step to the side, and her aunt moved the gun in her direction.

"Oh no, you don't," she said. "You're not going anywhere."

"Maybe not," she said, "but we can't just stand here. You can't shoot me in public like this."

"I can do anything I fucking want to."

A shout came from down the street. Her aunt froze and stared at Petra, shocked.

Petra shrugged her shoulders. "What did you expect?" She looked around, while she tried to keep an eye on her aunt because Migi held that gun steady on Petra. Her aunt was portly. Wider in the middle with skinny legs and a skinny top. But she was strong, even now. Even after all the years of not doing farm work, her aunt was still one of those inherently strong people.

Petra was five foot five and 118 pounds on a good day. She could run, and she could do yoga with ease, but she didn't inherit strength. Nothing like facing death head-on in order to give you a little bit more than you thought you had. She just had to have the perfect timing. More shouts came at the front of the house.

"Is Tristan expecting somebody else?" Petra asked in wonder.

"I doubt it. That was your uncle's voice," she replied, but she was distracted.

And, just like that, it was time. Petra took a quick jump forward and hit her aunt as hard as she could with her fist across Migi's jaw, as Petra grabbed her gun arm and shoved it up to the sky. Her aunt automatically pulled the trigger, firing harmlessly into the air. Migi went down under their combined weight, as she tripped backward, trying to avoid Petra. She heard her aunt struggling beneath her, but Petra straddled her aunt, holding down one of Migi's arms, as the woman hit her again and again. Finally Petra pulled back her fist and punched her aunt as hard as she could. With a hard, heavy groan, the older woman stopped struggling beneath her. Petra took a long slow breath and looked around. Nobody was around, nobody watching or nearby. She wasn't even sure what to do with that. It was all just a mess right now.

But, at the moment, she was alive and safe. She pulled the gun from her aunt's grasp, as Migi lay unconscious beneath her, then tucked it into the back of her own pants, just like Petra had seen on TV. It was foolish to imagine herself capable of handling it, but she wasn't a fool, and, if there was one thing she knew how to do, it was survive. Seems like she'd spent a lot of her life doing just that.

Sad as it may seem, life was all about what you did when shit was thrown at you. Did you buckle under the weight, or did you get up and create something for yourself? As she realized now, her aunt and uncle were both guilty of the former. They had buckled under the weight, and, as far as they were concerned, the world owed them a living, and they would take it, no matter who they hurt in the process. That was just incredible to Petra. If they would have put that energy into working, they would have been fine.

Petra had spent her life doing so much for them, thinking it was a family thing to do, only to discover that all they could think about was how to get her money. She'd never delved into the details of her father's estate because, in her mind, it was his and to be used only if she could get him care any other way. There had to be more to it. There had to be something more that she didn't know about.

Sure, they might have killed for that little bit in her father's account, that she'd added to with the proceeds from the sale of the house, but surely there was more to it than that. There had to be. She didn't want to think that her father's life and now hers was worth so little. But then, she was pretty sure that Cain would say that what was so little to Petra could be a lot to someone else. She didn't want to hear his logic right now. She wanted an answer that said secret millions were stacked away to have made all this even reasonably worthwhile.

But back to the present, now that her aunt was down and out, what would Petra do with Migi?

At that Petra smiled, pulled out her phone, and hit the number that Cain had told her to call. As soon as a woman answered, Petra identified herself and said, "Cain told me to contact you if there was a problem, but honestly I'm not sure what kind of problem this constitutes and whether you're the right person to talk to about it."

"Explain, please," said the crisp melodious voice on the other end.

Petra quickly explained about her aunt and what she learned.

"Good Lord," Ice said, "you really come from a nest of vipers, don't you?" but her tone was kind and relaxed.

"They're certainly not the people I thought they were, and that's difficult enough without all this other chaos."

"I'm sure it is," she said. "I'm already making calls. Somebody will be there to give you a hand in just a moment."

"I don't even have anything to tie her up with," she said.

"No, just sit tight and don't get off her. You stay exactly where you are."

"Will that help?" she asked, smiling.

"If she shows any signs of waking up, you hit her again, even harder," she was told. "That woman doesn't deserve anything but what she's got coming to her."

"I just hope I don't have to testify against her," she said.

"Well, if she does wake up, and you've got a handle on it, if she wants to confess some more and talk about things, it wouldn't hurt to get a recording of it."

"But that's easier said than done."

"I know," Ice said.

"I don't have anything other than my phone, and it wasn't on at the time. I'm sitting here, still waiting on Cain, and now I know my uncle is part of this. Plus, there were some shouts from the front of the house a while ago."

"I'm actually more concerned about somebody having heard your gunfire," Ice said smoothly. "Because that'll bring you unwanted visitors."

At that, she gasped, "I didn't think of that."

"Are you hidden?"

"We're on the ground behind a tree, but that's as far as it goes."

"Try to stay hidden, and let me know if anybody is coming toward you."

At Ice's statement, Petra hunkered even lower and looked around. "I can't really see anyone," she said.

"Unfortunately, in this case," she said, "you probably won't see anybody until they're already there."

The words sent chills down her spine. "I also haven't

heard from Cain."

"You leave Cain alone," she said. "He's a big boy."

"But these guys are mean. Just think about the things they've done," she said. "You might be used to more international-tourist type people, but these are your garden-variety sickos," she murmured.

With an obvious smile in her voice, Ice said, "Good description but unfortunately, in our world, we've seen plenty of them too."

"How do you handle it?" she asked curiously.

"One day at a time and cautiously," she said. "Any reason you're asking?"

Petra struggled, wondering whether she should say something, then finally opened up a bit. "It's just that something is between Cain and me," she said. "I don't really know what yet."

"If it's already there," she said, "chances are there isn't anything to question. It is what it is, and it's important."

"It is," she said, "but I don't quite understand how it happened so fast." A notable bewilderment carried in her voice.

"That's how it is with these guys," Ice said, chuckling. "The good news is that they're all solid heroes, aren't they?"

"Absolutely."

"They're good men to have at your side, and, if you're lucky enough to have one of them fall in love with you, you are blessed, indeed," Ice said, her voice warming.

"Well, it's a little early to say that," Petra said.

"I've known Cain a long time," Ice said. "He doesn't fall easily."

"I'm not even sure that he's falling," Petra said, backpedaling quickly. "I'm not exactly sure what we have here."

"Understood," Ice said, but she was still chuckling. "I suggest you enjoy the ride while you can."

"I just wonder what it'll take to get through this, so that we can find that out."

"Sit tight," she said. "We've got help coming."

Just then a vehicle pulled up along the back alley.

"A vehicle's behind me," she said, her voice dropping to a low whisper.

"Can you see the vehicle?"

"No," she said, "it's dark here."

"Good," she said. "With any luck it's my guy."

"How will I know?"

"Well, he'll start whistling as he walks toward you, for one thing," she said.

"And who is this guy?" she asked suspiciously. "I'm here holding a gun on an unconscious woman. It looks bad for me."

"Not in this case," she said. "I've had them open up the file on your father's accident from a couple years ago," she said smoothly. "And I've already given him a heads-up on what's happened right now."

Just then she heard whistling. "Okay, somebody's whistling," she said, "but I still can't be sure who it is."

"I'm glad you're cautious," she said. "I'll have him stop and identify himself." Just then the other guy stopped, and then he said, "Petra, my name is Antonio. I came to help. Ice sent me."

At that, she slowly stood from behind the trees and smiled. "Hi, I'm over here."

He nodded and came toward her.

She said, "I'm trying to stay out of sight of the house."

He quickly picked up the pace and ducked underneath

the tree beside her. "So, this is your aunt?"

"Yes," she said, "Unbeknownst to me, this bitch has caused me all kinds of trouble over the years, including trying to kill my father some time ago, resulting in him being deprived of oxygen and disabled thereafter. She says she didn't kill him yesterday, but my uncle said she did."

"We'll get to the bottom of it," he said. Glancing around, he said, "I understand there's an issue in the house too."

"Yes," she said, "but Ice told me to stay out of that."

"Absolutely," he said, "that's what these guys do."

"But everybody can run into trouble sometimes," she murmured.

He looked at her, smiled, and said, "Absolutely they can, but it's not necessarily something we should be looking at."

"I get it," she said. "I just don't like it."

He chuckled. "I'll take her out of here. Are you okay with that?"

"Definitely," she said, "as long as you don't bring her back again."

"Meaning, you don't want her loose again, is that it?"

"Yes. She's a hell of a danger to all of us."

"That she is," he said, "so that's not a problem." And in a smooth move that appeared effortless, this tall, dark stranger, who she'd never met before, bent down and hoisted her aunt up with his arms. "You won't see me again either."

"What about my aunt paying the price for her crimes?"

"No problem," he said. "That'll happen too. I'll just drop her off with someone who knows how to handle her."

"If you say so," she said, as she settled back under the tree. In a swift movement, he disappeared with her aunt in his arms. From her own phone came Ice's voice. "You okay?"

"Yes," she said, with a half sigh. "I'm okay. I can't really believe what just happened."

"Welcome to my world," Ice said in a dry tone. "We flip on a dime because the circumstances are like that."

"And what about Cain?"

"You keep asking about Cain," she said, with a smile. "What about Eton?"

"He went in after Eton," she said, "so I'm assuming they're both in there. But, yes, I'm more interested in Cain. Except I understand this is a way of life for all of you. How safe are they?"

"They have each other's backs. As you said, he went in after Eton. That's what our intel is saying too," she said. "So, we've got a team approaching, but I want to make sure you're out of there before they move in."

"I'm hidden in the back," she said. "I can just stay here."

"Not a good idea, when the bullets will start flying any-time now," she said.

"That's hardly fair," she said. "Cain told me to stay here. If I'm not here when he comes out, he—"

"I could always tell him where you are," she said. "I don't want you catching any of the loose gunfire."

"There's no such thing," she said, "as I'm slowly learn-ing. All these assholes intend to do everything they can. So they'll shoot to kill, right?"

"Yes, in this case, you've got people without a con-science," she said. "People who are only concerned about their needs and that alone."

"How does that even happen?" she asked.

"They get away with it once or twice, and then it be-comes easy, and they don't see any other way to live because anything else takes effort, and they're not into that."

"It's all BS," she murmured.

"In many ways, yes," Ice said, chuckling. "Still nothing you can do about it at the moment."

Petra said, "I want to make sure that Cain's okay. And, yes, Eton too. I'm not leaving this position because this is where Cain told me to be."

Ice hesitated but said, "If you say so." Then she quietly added, "What you need to do is get as low and as flat in a hiding spot as you can," she said, "because, when things start to break, it'll be all at once, and it'll be bad."

"If you say so," she said.

"Oh, I do," she murmured. "So hunker down, stay out of the way, and let us work."

"I wasn't planning on getting in the way," she protested.

"Not getting out of there," she said, "puts you inherently in the way. And I can't help that at all."

"Fine," she said. "I'll hunker down, but that's all I'll do."

CAIN PUSHED OPEN the door ever-so-slightly, and Tristan's voice got louder. Tristan had walked to the far end of the room. Cain peered through to see just where the man was and caught sight of Eton. He'd been beaten, and one side of his face was swollen and red. But his eyes looked hard and fierce. Tristan was at the far end—staring out the window—barking into the phone at somebody again. Cain gently pushed open the door and crept toward Eton. He crouched beside him and had him loose in seconds. As soon as he was done and started to move, Tristan's voice washed over him.

"You should have just shot me when you walked in," he said in an outrage. "What the hell? Did you think I wouldn't notice?"

"I didn't care if you noticed or not," Cain said, standing up, as Eton stood at the same time. He gave his legs and hands a shake, then turned to look at Tristan and said, "I owe you a couple punches."

"Like that'll happen," Tristan said, as he held up the handgun. "Did you guys not see this? Does it look like a toy to you?" But Tristan warily eyed the gun held at Cain's side.

"It's not enough to stop us," Cain said. "You might get one of us, but you sure as hell won't get us both."

"What? So it's okay for you guys to just lose one? How is that okay? I thought you guys were all about looking after each other," he said, staring at them in shock. "I can't believe you just walked in here and undid his ties."

"You were busy," Cain said, "so I didn't think to ask."

At that, Tristan raised the gun and fired, but both men moved out of the way. "This isn't some game," he said.

"No, it isn't," Cain said. "You came after friends of ours," he said. "We know all about it."

"You don't know jack," he said.

"We know that you hired Chico to come to the museum and take us down," he said, "and, of course, he failed by the way."

"I don't know anything about that," Tristan said, "and I don't hire idiots, but that one I did hire—we all make mistakes sometimes."

"Well, your biggest mistake was not making sure he'd done the job," he said, "because here we are."

"What? Am I supposed to be scared?"

"Not at all," he said. "I'd rather see you peeing in your pants right about now, but I can understand that the bravado hasn't quite given way to the reality of your current situation."

"Did you really think I was here alone?" he asked, almost shocked at the sound of his voice. Then he stopped and said, "Oh, what? Did you take out the old man?" He started to laugh. "That must have been a tough job."

"Why is that?"

"Well, he's not quite there you know. They're a pair and a half, those two. All they do is look around for opportunities to take people out and to steal from them." He shook his head. "They've been doing it for a long time."

"So I hear," Cain said. "Good thing Petra isn't like them."

"Sweet on her, are you?" He chuckled at that. "That sister was a loser too. The most clingy, needy thing you'll ever see, and, after she got pregnant the first time, I paid for the abortion, so she would get the hell out of my life, but, man, that didn't do it. She came back, always whining about how she shouldn't have gotten rid of her baby and how it had ruined her life and how it was up to me to fix it. What the hell? Am I some kind of magician who could fix her crazy ass?"

"I'm sure you could have done something."

"Well, she wanted me to get her pregnant again," he said. "Me or Chico, she didn't care which. But honestly I couldn't even be bothered with that. Killing her was an easy answer. I wasn't planning on ever coming back here. Imagine my surprise when I found out I had to." He shook his head. "That's just wrong."

"Leaving her here was wrong," Eton said. "And blaming your father for it."

"Well, there's another crazy old man. He knew what I'd done. He was the one who helped me get out, locking it from the inside. That's when he really started hitting the bottle apparently. He never could take the heat."

"Where, in your case, I suppose it wasn't about the heat as much as just ignoring what you didn't want to deal with, huh?"

"The old man wouldn't live forever. Especially once he started drinking, so whatever," he said. "It's not like her body would have gone anywhere."

"And what about your own sister? Any concern for her in this deal?"

"Shut up about my sister. If she isn't smart enough to get out, that's on her."

"So, you were just happy to let the body rot in that bedroom?"

"No, I would rather hide it somewhere else, but I had to book it just then. I was making plans, but I figured I'd leave it a year or two and then then deal with it."

"Jesus," he said.

"Oh, stop the judgment," Tristan said. "You've got no idea what it's like to live in this whorehouse of a town."

"No. You're quite right. I don't," Cain said.

"It's just a shithole," he said. "They're all freaking nuts. I mean, you met her aunt and uncle. You saw what they were like."

"I guess," he said. "I doubt they're all like that though."

"You'd be surprised," he said. "They're all just crazy, complete loony tunes."

"I wonder about that," Cain said.

"Wonder all you want," he said. "I don't owe you any explanations."

"No, you probably don't. But, at the same time, it would be nice if we could get an explanation," Cain said.

"Oh, so you want answers? That's too damn bad," he

snapped. "It's my world, not yours. You guys are done for it. I already sent off a message, looking for my backup."

Cain felt something inside hardening at the thought. Because, of course, he'd left Petra outside. "I don't think any backup's coming," he said. "I heard some shouting downstairs."

"Yeah, he was told to take out the old guy. I wanted to take out his wife myself though. That aunt is somebody who deserves a personal killing."

"Same as you," Cain said, and he walked to the window casually. Tristan glared at him and shouted, "Get the fuck away from the window," he said.

"Or what? You'll shoot me? Do you think nobody'll hear that? Didn't you see the crowd outside?"

Tristan gave him a startled look and walked to his window, looking carefully around the edge of the curtain and said, "What the—"

"Yeah, they're all here to see you."

"They've got nothing to see," he snapped. "What the hell did you guys do?"

"Well, a show like this deserves an audience," he said. "After all, you've got such a loving fan group here."

"They all fucking hate me," he said. "Why do you think I refused to come back?"

"Yeah, that's why you had to sneak in anytime you wanted guns, right? Maybe they have good reasons for hating you," Eton said. Suddenly Eton was already halfway across the room.

"Oh no, you don't," Tristan said, holding up the gun. "You just stop right there."

"And now we're back to that 'or what' thing," Eton replied.

"You're just looking for a bullet, aren't you? I'm happy to oblige."

"And that'll bring everybody in here," Cain said with a smile. "You see the cops out there too?"

At that, Tristan peered around the window and started to swear. "Jesus Christ," he said. "Are you fucking nuts? We don't need them here."

"Well, after they found the lovely present you left behind in that bedroom, I'm pretty sure they have a difference of opinion on that."

"It's not my fault," he said. "That woman was just a nasty nightmare."

"Now back to that whole 'the cops want to talk to you' thing."

"Nope, not these cops," he said, "I arranged for that to be fixed a long time ago."

"Yeah, but you probably didn't notice that a lot of changes have been made to the staff, and some other people have come in and taken a closer look at some of your allegiances."

He turned and glared. "Even if my buddies don't lie for me," he said, "they're still high up enough to make my life easier."

"Nope, not happening," Eton said with a smile. "So why don't you put down the gun and walk out carefully?"

"That'll never happen," he vowed.

"Well, I was hoping you might make it easier on yourself, but the cops are here, and they're just waiting," Cain said.

"Otherwise you'll stand up to us," Eton asked.

Tristan said, "I don't give a shit." But he was now more than a little disturbed and getting rattled, trying to engage both of them at once. "I should have just shot you when I caught you in here."

"Yep, you should have," Eton said, "but you didn't because you're a loser. You just wanted to make sure you got both members of the team."

"Well, if I don't get you, somebody else will," he said. "Failure is not an option in my world."

"Why is that?" Eton asked.

"Because somebody will take me out," he said. "I won't get a chance to stand trial."

"That's quite possible. So, what will you do? The cops might protect you, if you can incriminate the next in line."

"And that's just asking for a quick death penalty all of my own."

"But they'll do that anyway. You just said so," Eton argued. "So why not see them go down too?"

"Do you know anything about loyalty? Jesus Christ, how do you even survive in this pathetic world of yours? You can't go anywhere if you keep handing over your bosses."

"True enough," Eton said.

"Look, man," Cain said, "you've got about three choices. You can turn that gun on yourself, which I wouldn't mind," Cain said in a cheerful voice. "Or you can put down the gun. Or you can try to shoot it out with us," he said, "but it's not like we're not well armed ourselves." With that, he pulled out his second handgun and handed it to Eton.

Tristan started swearing heavily. "This isn't some game," he roared.

"No, it isn't," Cain said. "So make up your mind on what your next move will be." Both men held their guns pointed directly at him.

"You can die right now if you want," Eton said. "We

don't give a shit."

Tristan glared at them. He stood straight up, his back to the window, as he turned suddenly and looked out, as if wondering about jumping.

"Well, a jump will probably break both your legs," Cain said, "maybe even give you a few cracked ribs. Or maybe you'll end up paralyzed or have a brain injury. Then you can spend the rest of your life with somebody else taking care of you," he said. "Petra's aunt might be available."

Tristan turned, and, when the shot rang out, it didn't come from a direction anyone expected. But red bloomed across Tristan's chest, and a look of absolute shock came over his face, as he fell forward.

Instantly Cain raced to the window, keeping out of the line of sight, until he could peer through. A second shot blasted the window frame. He looked out as a truck took off on the far side of the road, and, even from where he stood, Cain saw it had no license plate. He pulled out his phone and quickly contacted Ice. "Black truck running away from the house right now. Looks like a Ford, a two-door Super-Cab, raised ever-so-slightly, no license plate. Shooter took Tristan out through the window. He's gone, taken out by his own guys. Tristan killed Morgan too."

"We'll see if we can find it on satellite. A hell of a crowd is outside your place as it is."

"I saw that. Your doing?"

"I think it might be your girlfriend's doing," she said, with a note of humor. "She was trying to figure out what she could do to help and to not get herself in trouble at the same time. I tried to get her out of there, but she insisted that you told her how she had to stay there, and she wasn't budging for nothing."

He chuckled. "Well, it's nice to know she can take orders when it's important."

"In my book, she's a keeper," Ice said cheerfully. "Don't screw it up."

She hung up, but her voice had been loud enough that Eton heard. He looked over, laughed, and said, "Yeah, don't screw it up."

Cain shook his head. "God dang it, people. If everybody would stay out of my business, it wouldn't be so bad," he muttered. As it was, he opened the window and called down to the cops, telling them to come up. He asked Eton, "You okay to handle this?"

"Yeah, you better go find Petra," he said. "I'm not exactly sure what the hell she's up to."

"Knowing her, I have no clue, but I suspect it'll be nothing but trouble."

"Well, now that will be your cross to bear," he said.

Cain stopped, looked at him, smiled, and said, "You know something about this cross? I'm thinking it's one I'd be totally happy to bear."

"You better do something about that blood before you get there."

At that, he looked at the steadily dripping blood on the floor. When the gunman fired the second shot to back Cain away from the window, flying debris had torn into the back of his hand and up into his arm. Splinters and glass had flown everywhere. While it didn't appear serious, it was definitely an injury that would require some attention.

At that, he disappeared, heading down to look for Petra. Ducking into a bathroom on the way, he grabbed a towel and wrapped it up to stop the bleeding.

He went out the back, and he stopped on the deck for a

long moment, as he searched the area to make sure it was safe. Then he raced to the trees where he'd left her. As soon as he got close, he called out to her. "Petra?"

Her head popped up through the canopy, and she smiled.

"It's over," he said, and he opened his arms.

She raced into his arms and hugged him tight. "Oh, my God," she said, "I was so worried when you didn't come out. Oh, no!" She gasped, when she saw the now bloody towel around his arm. "What happened?"

"I'm fine," he said, "and thank you for staying."

"Ice told me not to. She wanted me to leave, but I wouldn't."

"And that brings me to another question. Why did you contact Ice?"

She winced. "Well, I had a little problem, and I didn't know who else to call," she said. "My aunt tried to kill me."

He just stopped and stared.

She shrugged. "But I overpowered her," she said proudly, "and Ice sent somebody to help me."

"Good," he said with a big grin. "We actually had teams close by because this was all coming down."

"Right," she said.

"And while you were dealing with your aunt, I dealt with your uncle."

Petra's eyes widened.

Cain grabbed his phone, called Ice. "The uncle's tied up under Chico's bed. Can you tell the team? ... Thanks."

"So, if it's all over with, can we get the hell out of town now?"

"Maybe," he said, "but there is still your family."

"No," she said, "my family is done and gone. I'll need a

couple days to deal with things and to make final arrangements for my sister and my father. But, as for my aunt and my uncle?" She shook her head. "Not any family of mine."

"Well, that'll be a fun trial," he said. "Chances are you'll have to come back for that."

"And that thrills me to no end," she said sadly. "They killed so many people. We probably have no idea."

"I know, and I'm sorry. Sometimes you just get people who have absolutely no respect for human life."

"It's very sad," she said, "and I just don't get it."

"You don't have to anymore," he said, pulling her close.

She looked up at him and smiled. "Remember when you asked if I wanted to stay here or move away? Did you have a particular reason?"

"Let me put it this way," he said. "I'm heading back to Perth right now to run command central, as we figure out the next step." He pulled out Tristan's phone. "This is what I needed from Tristan—his contacts. He was killed, by the way—shot by one of his own men through the window."

She stared at him in shock. "You still don't know who's behind it all?"

"Not yet," he said, "but that's coming. And that's another reason why we're cleaning this up, then heading back to Perth, depending on what we find in this phone."

She looked behind his shoulder to see Eton coming down the steps. She smiled up at him. "I'm glad you're alive," she said simply. "But, if I were you, I would want to punch Tristan in the face a time or two for that."

"Not an issue," he said. "He took the ultimate bullet, and I'm good with that."

"Well, as long as he's dead and gone," she said, "but I would have liked to kick him myself for my sister."

"He did confess to that by the way," Cain said. "So that will help put your sister's case to rest."

She nodded ever-so-slightly. "It's all so sad."

"It is, but you have a chance to make a complete break," Eton said. "And you can help Cain not screw up this relationship." Then he turned, and, whistling happily, he walked out to the front.

"Help you not screw this up?" she asked.

"Don't worry about it. They're just bugging me. Everybody likes you, and they want me to not mess things up, so that you leave."

"Well, I was hoping to leave," she said and pulled back ever-so-slightly. "I was actually hoping to leave with you."

He looked at her in surprise, then drew her closer and said, "Looks like it's you and me now."

"Yeah," she said, "I figure we could use a few days to ourselves."

"It'll take a few days before we're cleared to leave," he warned.

"I know," she said, "but just even knowing that that's coming will be enough to get me through this."

"What did you have in mind?"

"I'm good with anything," she said. "I'll resign from my job, give notice on the apartment, and put everything in storage. I'll say goodbye to my family at the cemetery, and then I'll be free to rebuild something for myself, somewhere else. I don't know what form that'll take, but I know one thing," she said. "I'd really like to have you at my side."

He tilted her chin and kissed her gently. "And I would be honored," he said. "So let's go take care of business and see if we can shorten that time frame until we can get out of here. Or at least get it down to something more reasonable."

"First, we better get that arm of yours taken care of. I happen to have some contacts at the hospital. Maybe you can jump the line."

As it was, everything took longer than either of them wanted, but they managed to do an incredible amount in just a couple days. She buried both her father and her sister, cleaned out her apartment, and let go of her lease. She quit her job, while Cain and Eton raced around doing what they needed to do. She kept in touch, as she took care of the mundane details, and they took care of whatever was on their list.

They hadn't really filled her in on too much of it, but she knew they were looking for whatever was the next step in this journey. They were trying to find the shooter who'd killed Tristan but figured it was just another hired hand. They focused on tracking down every number in Tristan's phone, trying to find the next connection. Last thing she'd heard was something about Switzerland. She was totally okay with Switzerland, but Eton didn't like the idea at all.

Cain ended up having some out-patient surgery to repair the damage to his arm and would have some rehab to do once it was healed. But finally he was on the mend, and she had finished with the police, the funerals, and her apartment. The last of the furniture was being loaded into a truck to be donated to a local charity. "Do you realize I only have what's in the car now?" she murmured. "Everything else is gone. Even my car can be sold later, if need be."

"You have what counts," he said. "You have your memories. I think it was smart to deal with it all, rather than cram it in a storage unit and have to come back."

She smiled and nodded. "I do too. It feels kind of freeing in a way. I have a whole new life ahead of me."

"Only if you're ready for it," he said.

"I am," she said.

He smiled and reached to hug her. "Well, come on then. We're booked at a hotel about four hours from here. I didn't want to go too far on the first day, in case you were emotional."

"I am emotional," she said, holding back tears, "but it's all good."

And, sure enough, it was. He was driving her car, his injuries still sore, but definitely better.

CHAPTER 15

W HEN THEY PULLED into the bed-and-breakfast, it was four and a half hours later. She looked up and said, "What are we doing about dinner?"

"A little restaurant is around the corner," he said. "Let's go check in first." They checked into the bed-and-breakfast and moved into their room. She stopped in the doorway, noting the huge bed, and gave him a sideways look. He just smiled and said, "No pressure."

"On you or on me?"

He gave a bark of laughter at that. "Come on. Let's go get dinner," he said. "We have the rest of our lives to talk about how many bedrooms we need."

"As long as the rest of our lives means that we're coming back here sometime in the next hour, I'm good," she said. He squeezed her fingers, and they headed for the restaurant. But the whole time he could feel the need coursing through him, knowing that big bed was there, waiting for them. The knowledge that she was just as eager for him as he was for her made dinner almost a torment.

"Do you think we can take it and leave?" she muttered some twenty minutes later, when they still hadn't been served. He looked at her and smiled.

"Why not?" When the waiter passed by again, Cain called him over and asked if they could get it to go. The waiter immediately apologized for the delay and said it was almost ready.

"Good," he said. "So if you could have them pack it up, that would be perfect." And that's what they did. They were standing outside with their dinner, when he looked at her. "That's not quite what I expected to happen."

"You should have," she said, with energy. "Come on. Let's go." And, with that, they headed back to the bed-and-breakfast with their dinner in tow. As soon as they got into their bedroom, she took the bags from him and carefully put them down on the small table and said, "I don't know about you, but I'm really hungry."

But then she turned and faced him, gave him a cheeky smile, and started taking off her clothes. His breath caught, and he was flabbergasted, as, within seconds, she stood before him completely nude.

"Dear God," he murmured, his eyes feasting on her.

"And you," she said, "are definitely overdressed." His hands got busy, but she brushed him away and quickly undid his shirt and his belt buckle. Only she wasn't willing to give him any time to get his clothes off, as her hands slipped across his skin, stroking and discovering, but, when she lowered her head and nipped him on the collarbone, he let out a muffled roar and started stripping as fast as he could.

"What's the rush?" she murmured.

"You," he said, breathing hard. But she chuckled, and he quickly snagged her up, carried her to the bed, both of them now completely nude. He came down on top of her, and immediately she moaned, arched her back, rubbing up against him, and wiggled ever-so-slightly, sliding skin against skin, heat against heat.

"Oh, my God," she said, "I've wanted this since the first time I saw you." She wrapped her arms around his neck, pulled him down tight, and kissed him hard. He leaned into the kiss, his body already more than ready, hitting the flashpoint sooner than he would have liked, but she was just incredible. She was so honest and so giving that he knew he couldn't hold back. He tried to pull away his head, but she was having none of it. Her tongue slipped into a war with his, even as her hand slid down to grab his buttocks. When her nails dug into his flesh, he reared back slightly, but, when he came back, it was to find her thighs wide and her long legs wrapped tight around his hips.

He slipped inside, shuddering at the heavy emotions coursing through him. He pulled back, buried his face against the crook of her neck, and just tried to control his breathing. Again, she wasn't having any of it. She clamped down on him tight. "I need you so much," she whispered. "I've wanted you for so long. I want this, and I want this now." She placed her hands on either side of his face and kissed him long and deep, as her hips started to move.

He pulled his head back, hitting the snapping point, and started to plow and plunge deep into her. It was already past the point of no control, and he knew there was only a slim chance of getting her to catch up with him. But, when he looked down to see her mouth open, her eyes closed, and her face a picture of absolute joy, he wondered how he'd gotten so lucky. She reached up, clung to him, and whispered, "Now, now, now." When he plunged one more time, she bucked beneath him and cried out.

He watched, trying desperately to hold back his own joy to see her reaction as she soared over the edge, a tiny film of sweat breaking over her face as her relief swept through her.

And then it was over for him too, and he groaned a heavy deep guttural roar of release himself, before he collapsed on the bed. He gasped for air, trying to regain his balance.

She murmured, "Now that's the kind of meal I enjoy. I was really hungry."

He burst out laughing and cuddled her close.

"This is what our life should be like," she said. "Passion, joy, and laughter."

He opened his eyes, looked down at her, and said, "Absolutely. Promise me more nights like tonight?"

"I promise," she said, "Lots more. Forever and a day. Wait. That's not fair," she said. "It's not fair to pin you down like that."

"Forever and a day," he said.

With a nod, she smiled and kissed him deeply. "Anytime you're ready to go again, I'm still a little hungry."

He smiled, rolled over, and kissed her again. Life had never been better.

EPILOGUE

ETON DURAM STUDIED the phone numbers in his hand. Switzerland, but where in Switzerland? It might be a small country, but it wasn't that small. Finally he got a phone call from Kano.

"Garret is awake!"

"I knew that," he said. "So what's up?"

"Ah," and then there was an awkward silence and a rustling noise. A different voice came on the phone.

"He means that I'm here now, and I'm, like, really awake."

"You're supposed to be in the hospital," Eton said immediately. "What the hell are you doing here?"

"I'm not technically *here*. I'm in Switzerland, waiting for you to get your ass over here."

"Where in Switzerland though?" he said. "I was just looking at that."

"Outside of Geneva is my best bet, but I think we'll end up in Baden soon enough."

"Do we have anything to go on?"

"Oh, yeah," Garret said. "I'll send the info through, but get on your flight and get the hell here."

"I'm not booked anywhere yet," he said.

"Well, check your email," he said, "because you actually are. And you're flying out in about an hour and ten minutes.

Get your ass over here. We've got work to do."

Eton stared down at his phone to check his email, and, sure enough, his flights were booked for Geneva. He shook his head, sent a text message to Garret. **You should be in the hospital.**

No fucking way. I've been there long enough. It's time for me to get after these assholes, so I'm getting after them with you. Cain needs to rest up and rehab that arm, so now it's our turn.

Eton agreed entirely. Not to mention the fact that Cain was working hard on not messing up his relationship with Petra. Eton grinned at that because, if anybody deserved to have a good relationship, it was Cain. He was the kind of guy who gave his heart and soul to a cause and so very often didn't get anything back out of it, except the satisfaction of a job well done. That's what was most important, sure, but it still didn't change the fact that sometimes a guy needed a little bit more. And, in this case, Cain sure as hell did. But he got it, and that was all good.

Eton really liked Petra; she was something else. Somewhat wistfully, he thought about Ryland and Cain, and Eton wondered if it would ever be his turn to find that someone special. When the hotel's front desk called, he checked his watch.

"Your cab is here."

Smiling, he told them that he'd be right down. As always, Kano had thought of everything. And whether it was Kano or Garret, Eton was damn glad to have his team behind him and on board, as part of his mission. It was one thing to have somebody to watch his back; it was another thing to know they were your brothers and were looking out for your best interests too. And they had the best team possible. The loss of Bullard was hard to take, but, after all these days, it was hard to imagine he had lived somehow. Eton just had to make sure nobody else would go down because of these assholes. Enough was enough. It was time to end this, and he was the guy to do it.

This concludes Book 2 of Bullard's Battle: Cain's Cross.

Read about Eton's Escape: Bullard's Battle, Book 3

Eton's Escape: Bullard's Battle (Book #3)

Welcome to a new stand-alone but interconnected series from Dale Mayer. This is Bullard's story—and that of his team's. All raw, rough, incredibly capable men who have one goal: to find out who was behind the attack on their leader, before the attacker, or attackers, return to finish the job.

Stay tuned for more nonstop action as the men narrow down their suspects ... and find a way to let love back into their own empty lives.

Eton journeys to Switzerland, unimpressed at finding Garret there as his backup. Barely recovered but pissed and mobile, Garret refuses to be kept out of service any longer. Eton's intel leads them to a small village, to a woman in distress, and to someone who likes cleaning up a trail a little too much.

Living a quiet life with her aging father, Sammy is surprised by an offer of help when she gets an unexpected flat tire. Strangers in this area are not common, and neither are they well received. Still this stranger's a can-do person, and she instinctively turns to him when she soon needs additional help.

Only to find he's partly why she's in trouble—and he's got bigger troubles of his own. Now they both had to get out of this nightmare and somewhere safe and sound, ... before it's too late.

Find Book 2 here!

To find out more visit Dale Mayer's website.

smarturl.it/DMSCain

Damon's Deal: Terkel's Team (Book #1)

Welcome to a brand-new connected series of intrigue, betrayal, and ... murder, from the *USA Today* best-selling author Dale Mayer. A series with all the elements you've come to love, plus so much more... including psychics!

A betrayal from within has Terkel frantic to protect those he can, as his team falls one by one, from a murderous killer he helped create.

I CE POURED HERSELF a coffee and sat down at the compound's massive dining room table with the others. When her phone rang, she smiled at the number displayed. "Hey, Terk. How're you doing?" She put the call on Speakerphone.

"I'm okay," Terkel said, his voice distracted and tight.

"Terk?" Merk called from across the table. He got up and walked closer and sat across from Levi. "You don't sound too good, brother. What's up?"

"I'm fine," Terk said. "Or I will be. Right now, things are blown to shit."

"As in literally?" Merk asked.

"The entire group," Terk said, "they're all gone. I had a solid team of eight, and they're all gone."

"Dead?"

Several others stood to join them, gathered around Ice's phone. Levi stepped forward, his hand on Ice's shoulder. "Terk? Are they all dead?"

"No." Terk took a deep breath. "I'm not making sense. I'm sorry."

"Take it easy," Ice said, her voice calm and reassuring. "What do you mean, *they're all gone?*"

"All their abilities are gone," he said. "Something's happened to them. Somebody has deliberately removed whatever super senses they could utilize—or what we have been utilizing for the last ten years for the government." His tone was bitter. "When the US gov recently closed us down, they promised that our black ops department would never rise again, but I didn't expect them to attack us personally."

"What are you talking about?" Merk said in alarm, standing up now to stare at Ice's phone. "Are you in danger?"

"Maybe? I don't know," Terk said. "I need to find out exactly what the hell's going on."

"What can we do to help?" Ice asked.

Terk gave a broken laugh. "That's not why I'm calling. Well, it is, but it isn't."

Ice looked at Merk, who frowned, as he shook his head. Ice knew he and the others had heard Terk's stressed out tone and the completely confusing bits and pieces coming from his mouth. Ice said, "Terk, you're not making sense again. Take a breath and explain. Please. You're scaring me."

Terk took a long slow deep breath. "Tell Stone to open the gate," he said. "She's out there."

"Who's out there?" Levi asked, hopped up, looked outside, and shrugged.

"She's coming up the road now. You have to let her in."

"Who? Why?"

"*Because*," he said, "she's also harnessed with C-4."

"Jesus," Levi said, bolting to display the camera feeds to the big screen in the room. "Is it live?"

"It is, and she's been sent to you."

"Well, that's an interesting move," Ice said, her voice sharp, activating her comm to connect to Stone in the control room. "Who's after us?"

"I think it's rebels within the Iranian government. But it could be our own government. I don't know anymore," Terk snapped. "I also don't know how they got her so close to you. Or how they pinned your connection to me," he said. "I've been very careful."

"We can look after ourselves," Ice said immediately. "But who is this woman to you?"

"She's pregnant," he said, "so that adds to the intensity here."

"Understood. So who is the father? Is he connected somehow?"

There was silence on the other end.

Merk said, "Terk, talk to us."

"She's carrying my baby," Terk replied, his voice heavy.

Merk, his expression grim, looked at Ice, her face mirroring his shock. He asked, "How do you know her, Terk?"

"Brother, you don't understand," Terk said. "I've never met this woman before in my life." And, with that, the phone went dead.

Find Book 1 here!

To find out more visit Dale Mayer's website.

smarturl.it/DMSTTDamon

Author's Note

Thank you for reading Cain's Cross: Bullard's Battle, Book 2! If you enjoyed the book, please take a moment and leave a short review.

Dear reader,

I love to hear from readers, and you can contact me at my website: www.dalemayer.com or at my Facebook author page. To be informed of new releases and special offers, sign up for my newsletter or follow me on BookBub. And if you are interested in joining Dale Mayer's Reader Group, here is the Facebook sign up page.
https://smarturl.it/DaleMayerFBGroup

Cheers,
Dale Mayer

Get THREE Free Books Now!

Have you met the SEALS of Honor?

SEALs of Honor Books 1, 2, and 3. Follow the stories of brave, badass warriors who serve their country with honor and love their women to the limits of life and death.

Read Mason, Hawk, and Dane right now for FREE.

Go here and tell me where to send them!
http://smarturl.it/EthanBofB

About the Author

Dale Mayer is a *USA Today* best-selling author, best known for her SEALs military romances, her Psychic Visions series, and her Lovely Lethal Garden cozy series. Her contemporary romances are raw and full of passion and emotion (Broken But ... Mending series). Her thrillers will keep you guessing (By Death series), and her romantic comedies will keep you giggling (*It's a Dog's Life*, a stand-alone novella; and the Broken Protocols series, starring Charming Marvin, the cat).

Dale honors the stories that come to her—and some of them are crazy and break all the rules and cross multiple genres!

To go with her fiction, she also writes nonfiction in many different fields, with books available on résumé writing, companion gardening, and the US mortgage system. She has recently published her Career Essentials series. All her books are available in print and ebook format.

Connect with Dale Mayer Online

Dale's Website – www.dalemayer.com
Twitter – @DaleMayer
Facebook – facebook.com/DaleMayer.author
BookBub – bookbub.com/authors/dale-mayer

Also by Dale Mayer

Published Adult Books:

Bullard's Battle
Ryland's Reach, Book 1
Cain's Cross, Book 2
Eton's Escape, Book 3
Garret's Gambit, Book 4
Kano's Keep, Book 5
Fallon's Flaw, Book 6
Quinn's Quest, Book 7
Bullard's Beauty, Book 8
Bullard's Best, Book 9

Terkel's Team
Damon's Deal, Book 1

Kate Morgan
Simon Says… Hide, Book 1

Hathaway House
Aaron, Book 1
Brock, Book 2
Cole, Book 3
Denton, Book 4

The K9 Files

Lovely Lethal Gardens

Psychic Vision Series

Tuesday's Child

Hide 'n Go Seek

Maddy's Floor

Garden of Sorrow

Knock Knock...

Rare Find

Eyes to the Soul

Now You See Her

Shattered

Into the Abyss

Seeds of Malice

Eye of the Falcon

Itsy-Bitsy Spider

Unmasked

Deep Beneath

From the Ashes

Stroke of Death

Ice Maiden

Snap, Crackle...

Psychic Visions Books 1–3

Psychic Visions Books 4–6

Psychic Visions Books 7–9

By Death Series

Touched by Death

Haunted by Death

Chilled by Death

By Death Books 1–3

Broken Protocols – Romantic Comedy Series

Cat's Meow

Cat's Pajamas

Cat's Cradle

Cat's Claus

Broken Protocols 1-4

Broken and... Mending

Skin

Scars

Scales (of Justice)

Broken but... Mending 1-3

Glory

Genesis

Tori

Celeste

Glory Trilogy

Biker Blues

Morgan: Biker Blues, Volume 1

Cash: Biker Blues, Volume 2

SEALs of Honor

Mason: SEALs of Honor, Book 1

Hawk: SEALs of Honor, Book 2

Dane: SEALs of Honor, Book 3

Swede: SEALs of Honor, Book 4

Shadow: SEALs of Honor, Book 5

Cooper: SEALs of Honor, Book 6

Heroes for Hire

Levi's Legend: Heroes for Hire, Book 1

Stone's Surrender: Heroes for Hire, Book 2

Merk's Mistake: Heroes for Hire, Book 3

Rhodes's Reward: Heroes for Hire, Book 4

Flynn's Firecracker: Heroes for Hire, Book 5

Logan's Light: Heroes for Hire, Book 6

Harrison's Heart: Heroes for Hire, Book 7

Saul's Sweetheart: Heroes for Hire, Book 8

Dakota's Delight: Heroes for Hire, Book 9

Michael's Mercy (Part of Sleeper SEAL Series)

Tyson's Treasure: Heroes for Hire, Book 10

Jace's Jewel: Heroes for Hire, Book 11

Rory's Rose: Heroes for Hire, Book 12

Brandon's Bliss: Heroes for Hire, Book 13

Liam's Lily: Heroes for Hire, Book 14

North's Nikki: Heroes for Hire, Book 15

Anders's Angel: Heroes for Hire, Book 16

Reyes's Raina: Heroes for Hire, Book 17

Dezi's Diamond: Heroes for Hire, Book 18

Vince's Vixen: Heroes for Hire, Book 19

Ice's Icing: Heroes for Hire, Book 20

Johan's Joy: Heroes for Hire, Book 21

Galen's Gemma: Heroes for Hire, Book 22

Zack's Zest: Heroes for Hire, Book 23

Bonaparte's Belle: Heroes for Hire, Book 24

Heroes for Hire, Books 1–3

Heroes for Hire, Books 4–6

Heroes for Hire, Books 7–9

Heroes for Hire, Books 10–12

Heroes for Hire, Books 13–15

SEALs of Steel

Badger: SEALs of Steel, Book 1

Erick: SEALs of Steel, Book 2

Cade: SEALs of Steel, Book 3

Talon: SEALs of Steel, Book 4

Laszlo: SEALs of Steel, Book 5

Geir: SEALs of Steel, Book 6

Jager: SEALs of Steel, Book 7

The Final Reveal: SEALs of Steel, Book 8

SEALs of Steel, Books 1–4

SEALs of Steel, Books 5–8

SEALs of Steel, Books 1–8

The Mavericks

Kerrick, Book 1

Griffin, Book 2

Jax, Book 3

Beau, Book 4

Asher, Book 5

Ryker, Book 6

Miles, Book 7

Nico, Book 8

Keane, Book 9

Lennox, Book 10

Gavin, Book 11

Shane, Book 12

Diesel, Book 13

Jerricho, Book 14

The Mavericks, Books 1–2

The Mavericks, Books 3–4

The Mavericks, Books 5–6

The Mavericks, Books 7–8

The Mavericks, Books 9–10

The Mavericks, Books 11–12

Collections

Dare to Be You…

Dare to Love…

Dare to be Strong…

RomanceX3

Standalone Novellas

It's a Dog's Life

Riana's Revenge

Second Chances

Published Young Adult Books:

Family Blood Ties Series

Vampire in Denial

Vampire in Distress

Vampire in Design

Vampire in Deceit

Vampire in Defiance

Vampire in Conflict

Vampire in Chaos

Vampire in Crisis

Vampire in Control

Vampire in Charge

Family Blood Ties Set 1–3

Family Blood Ties Set 1–5

Family Blood Ties Set 4–6

Family Blood Ties Set 7–9

Sian's Solution, A Family Blood Ties Series Prequel
   Novelette

Design series

Dangerous Designs

Deadly Designs

Darkest Designs

Design Series Trilogy

Standalone

In Cassie's Corner

Gem Stone (a Gemma Stone Mystery)

Time Thieves

Published Non-Fiction Books:

Career Essentials

Career Essentials: The Résumé

Career Essentials: The Cover Letter

Career Essentials: The Interview

Career Essentials: 3 in 1

Made in the USA
Middletown, DE
13 May 2021

39635831R00129